Book 4 o

Ana Stilwell

Mystery of the Dead Man's Dare

J.W. Jenkins

GreenTree Publishers
Newnan, GA

Ana Stilwell – Mystery of the Dead Man's Dare

The characters and events of this book are fictitious. Any similarity to real persons, living or dead, is coincidental and not intended by the author.

Copyright © 2021 by J. W. Jenkins

All rights reserved. No part of this publication may be reproduced, stored in a retrieval system, or transmitted by any means – electronic, mechanical, photographic (photocopying), recording, or otherwise – without prior permission in writing from the author.

Printed in the United States of America

ISBN-13: 978-1-944483-46-3

Follow J. W. Jenkins on social media:

Facebook: @anastilwellbooks

Instagram: @anastilwellcollection

Website: www.AnaStilwell.com

Email: Anastilwell2019@gmail.com

Greentree Publishers:
www.greentreepublishers.com

Dedication

I dedicate *Ana Stilwell: Mystery of the Dead Man's Dare* to our grandchildren: Mackenna, Nathan, Katie, T.J., Maggie, Caroline, Davis, Amy, Charlotte, Bethany, and Christian. Sharing stories with them inspired this journey.

Special Thanks

To my amazing and very patient wife, Pam. There is no way I could write these books without her. What a precious gift of God she is!

To Adele Brinkley, Diana Fowler, Jayden Pope, June Black, Ayerl Lawrence, and Chuck Witcher who provided valued editing assistance.

To Dr. Tim Riordan, of Greentree Publishers. He is a such a great friend and continues to teach me so much. Check out his books featured on the last pages of this and other Ana Stilwell books.

As a special

THANK YOU

for purchasing

ANa StiLWeLL

Mystery of the Dead Man's Dare

I would like to email you a *free* diagram (.pdf) of

Ana Stilwell's mansion!

Send your request to:

anastilwell2019@gmail.com

J.W. Jenkins

What's happened so far in the Ana Stilwell Mystery Series?

Book One
ANa StiLWeLL'S GreateSt AdVeNtUre
She's eleven and has an annoying younger brother. Her family just moved to Lewistowne, so she's in a new school. While exploring the creek behind their house, Ana finds an old, stone wall that belongs to the abandoned Griffin estate. Driven by a determined curiosity, she deciphers a trail of clues that lead her to a amazing, life-changing discovery.

Book Two
ANa StiLWeLL - MySterieS oF tHe MaNSioN
As new owner of the Griffin estate, multi-millionaire Ana is determined make things right. She also wants to learn if the huge mansion holds other hidden secrets.
But even Ana is not prepared for what she finds.

Book Three
ANa StiLWeLL - THe LigHt iN tHe ToWer
After making several very startling discoveries in the mansion, Ana knows that she can't stop until she has the answer to her biggest question of all. And this time...she's not alone.

Ana Stilwell
Mystery of the Dead Man's Dare
Who's who?

- Andrew Collins – Ana's huge bodyguard
- Chuck Switcher – her lawyer and financial advisor
- Connor Stilwell – her younger brother
- Nancy Stilwell – Ana's mother
- Ronnie Stilwell – her father
- Courtney Thompson – Ana's Sunday School teacher
- Carter Hudson – her very close friend
- Skylar Perkins – a mean girl from school
- Dr. David Barnes – her pastor
- Olivia Freeman, Maggie Benson, Amy Edwards, Bethany Green, Charlotte Howard, Katie Strong, Caroline Jensen, & Mackenna Myers – Ana's Sunday School classmates
- Diane Davis – the lady restoring the mansion
- Antonio D'Amico – an art expert
- Margaret Williams – a professional chef
- LeeAnn Fendley – the chef's assistant
- Lawrence Hill – Rudolph Griffin's attorney
- Rudolph Griffin – the wealthy, deceased owner of the Griffin estate and mansion
- Beatrice Griffin – his beautiful, deceased wife
- Captain Lewis Griffin – their only son who died a hero in the Vietnam War
- And, of course, Ricky!

Chapter One

Ana Stilwell read the hand-scrawled message one more time. Holding it closer to her face, she studied the odd drawing to guess what it might be.

"What cha' got there?" Andrew's voice cracked like unexpected thunder two inches from her right ear, but she didn't flinch. Thankfully, Ana had glimpsed her enormous bodyguard sneaking up from behind, so his attempt to make her leap out of her skin had failed…this time.

"You're pretty entertaining. You know that?"

"I think so." His huge head was still right next to hers. "So, what is it?"

Ana glared at him and stuck the card in his face.

"You tell me, Detective Collins." The almost sarcastic tone in her voice was to let him know she did not appreciate him trying to startle her. Andrew didn't take the hint.

"Detective Collins?" He took the card and wagged it at her. "Did you know that when I was on the police force, I was a real detective for almost two months?" Lifting his nose into the air, he continued, "I got the highest marks on my exam. The chief said I was a natural." He cast a questioning stare at the twelve-year old multi-millionaire. "Were you aware of that?" Ana didn't respond or look at him.

Chuck Switcher, her lawyer, financial advisor, and now, trusted friend, was seated a few feet away. "That was one of the main reasons why she wanted me to hire *you*," he told Andrew. They both turned and looked at Ana.

"Good grief," she said, rolling her eyes. "Why did you have to tell him that?"

"Really?" Andrew puffed out his chest. "You hired me for my detective skills?"

"I need a drink of water," she groaned. After fishing a bottle out of the melting ice, Ana closed the lid to the plastic cooler and wandered over to the edge of the large, white tent. She had promised her younger brother, Connor, a spectacular birthday celebration, and she was keeping her word.

Spread out across the manicured lawn of the fabulous Griffin Estate, which now belonged to her, was an assortment of inflatables: several slides, one of them almost three stories high, a basketball court, a challenging obstacle course, and a very large castle complete with a drawbridge. As Ana unscrewed the cap off the bottle, she noticed the "T" in the Lewistowne Party Service logo.

Party Service

Now, isn't that clever? It's a large party tent.

Ana took a long drink of water and thought about the mysterious drawing on the card.

Why couldn't it be that simple?

Connor and a herd of his "best" friends were running, sliding, and shouting at the top of their lungs. The table to her right was covered with gifts. Ronnie Stilwell, Ana's father, was busy stuffing a large black trash bag with the gift-wrapping Connor had violently ripped off his presents. Ana's mother, Nancy, was busy cleaning up the table where just minutes before a delicious caramel fudge birthday cake had glowed with nine candles. A stack of clear containers now waited on the leftovers.

Surveying the scene in front of her, Ana's gaze halted on the imitation castle. Bouncing around inside with a bunch of kids used to be a lot of fun, but not now. Not anymore. Not after Austria. Closing her eyes, she remembered sitting in the plane, flying above the clouds with Carter Hudson and how it felt as the plane touched down in Vienna, and came to a stop five thousand miles away from Lewistowne. Scenes of the fascinating European capital, the quaint villages, and gorgeous countryside came into focus. Ana drew in another deep, long breath, let it out slowly, and relaxed for the first time in weeks.

It's like I'm right there!

As she rubbed the cool plastic of the bottle against her cheek, another world and a completely different lifestyle took shape in her mind. Once again, she stood on the balcony of the medieval castle—that had almost been hers—and gazed across the vast expanse of the wondrous Danube River valley. Ana's very vivid imagination kicked in.

I would have been Anastasia Elisabeth Stilwell of Castle Greifenstein.

She took another sip of water and chuckled, "Well, what do you know?" It was the first time Ana could remember actually liking her real name. Without trying, another delightfully wonderful consideration caused the corners of her mouth to curl upwards into a satisfying grin. In her mind, she was still on the balcony, but now she was not alone anymore.

What about Anastasia Elisabeth Hudson?

A blood-curdling shriek ripped her away from her delicious daydreaming. She could tell her brother wasn't hurt just mad. After nine years, she knew all of his sounds by heart.

"You are it!" Connor bellowed at the top of his lungs. "I got you on the arm!"

"Uh, uh! You only got my sleeve!" objected his best friend, Johnny Ralston. Ana watched as the other boys quickly formed a circle around them. A lively discussion commenced as to what counted as a valid *tag*. Finally, Connor huffed, stepped forward, jammed his finger into Johnny's chest, and glared at the others.

"It's my birthday party, so you all have to do what I say!"

The impact of invoking this supreme edict of birthday party protocol caused the other boys to immediately end the argument, turn on Johnny, and pronounce that he was "it." The chasing and screaming resumed. Ana drained the last mouthful of water from the bottle.

Hopefully, he'll sleep like a rock tonight.

"See if you can sniff this out." Andrew read the message loudly enough for her to hear him. Ana whirled around and went back to where he and Chuck were sitting. He looked at her. "What do you think this squiggly drawing is?"

She shook her head. "Something that's going to drive me nuts until I can figure it out."

Andrew glanced over at Chuck. "And you're sure it's from Rudolph Griffin?"

5

"It was in this small envelope with her name on it. See how shaky the handwriting is? It's just like on the note." Chuck held out the envelope toward Andrew. "I found it in the manila envelope with the new will."

"When I was in his bedroom," explained Ana. "I pulled out the new will and looked at it. Then I put it back into the envelope." She pointed at the object in Chuck's hand. "I'm positive that little envelope was not in there."

"Then he had to have written it after she left," said Chuck. "He put it with the will, knowing she would find it. Griffin must have realized that he didn't have long to live."

"That makes sense," agreed Andrew. He held up the card again. "Why do you think he capitalized the word SNIFF?" Chuck shook his head.

"I don't have the faintest idea, but it's definitely a clue."

"Yeah, but to what?" Andrew gave the card to Ana.

She watched as he paced back and forth.

"It could be anything," muttered Chuck.

"Okay." Andrew halted directly in front of her. "Rudolph Griffin figured you had to be smart because, first, you found his will when no one else could, and then, second, you found him! So, whatever this is," he said, pointing at the card in her hand, "it's got to be a real doozy." He looked at Chuck. "If you ask me, this sounds more like some kind of a challenge, or…a dare." Ana stared at the card and then back up at the two men.

"Yeah. A dead man's dare."

Chapter Two

After all of Connor's guests were finally gone, the crew from the party service began folding up chairs and tables. Ana and Andrew helped load the presents, leftovers, cooler, and bags full of trash into Chuck's truck and her dad's SUV.

"I can follow you to your house and help you with all of this," Ana overheard Chuck tell her parents, "but then I've got to make a quick run into town." She saw him wink at Andrew. "Which means..." Chuck screwed up his face like someone does before they share bad news.

"That Ana and I get to deal with *birthday boy* over there." Andrew motioned with his head toward Connor who was frantically racing from one inflatable to the next as he tried to get in as many last jumps as possible.

Almost pleading, Ana's mother asked, "You don't mind, do you?"

"Of course not," said Andrew. Ana saw Connor run to the blowup castle and disappear through the door in the fake drawbridge. She bit her bottom lip.

That's easy for you to say. You won't be the one who will have to go in there after him.

At *Pizza World*, it was always her job to wade into the huge ball pit, snag her wiggly, screaming brother, and drag him out. Ana wrinkled her nose as she stared at the castle.

I'll bet it stinks like sweaty little boys in there.

After taking down the large white tent and packing it away in the truck, one of the crew walked over to the largest slide and turned a knob on the powerful blower that converted it into a vacuum. Almost instantly, the huge inflatable began to cave in on itself. Ana's mother got Andrew's attention.

"If it's possible, would you ask them to please take down the castle last? Connor seems to like it the best."

"Sure thing." Andrew jogged over and relayed the message. Ana saw the man say something in return and nod. Connor must have heard them, too, because the castle began to shake even more violently.

He's banging around in there like a squirrel.

Suddenly, the castle stopped quivering. Ana saw her brother poke his head out through the drawbridge opening to check on the workers' progress.

Andrew rejoined the group. "They said it won't be a problem. The castle is always the last thing to go into the truck."

"Maybe they'll roll him up inside it," muttered Ana under her breath. She hadn't meant for anyone to hear her, but they all did.

"Ana!" scolded her mother.

"I was just kidding!"

Everyone stared at her, so Ana glared back at them with that embarrassed, wide-eyed stare that girls make when they are caught saying something, that they shouldn't have but are not truly sorry about it. After a brief awkward silence, everyone erupted with laughter.

Moments later, Ana's parents and Chuck were finally ready to leave. Her mother rolled down the window as the car inched forward.

"See you back at the house."

Ana waved but didn't say anything. The day was gorgeous. In the distance she could see her tennis courts. Closer to the right, the water of her Olympic-sized swimming pool sparkled beneath a brand-new diving board. The freshly painted pool house with inviting chairs and shadow-spending cabanas was expertly accented with attractive trees, shrubs, plants, and flowers. The restoration crew had finished only the day before. Ana was glad she had decided against throwing Connor a pool party and opted for inflatables instead.

"I'll go check on Master Stilwell," said Andrew and headed back toward the party area. "I don't want him getting in their way."

"Good idea!" said Ana. "I'm going to stroll around and see how everything looks."

Walking backwards, he called, "Don't take too long."

"I won't."

Ana made her way toward the front of her mansion. The rhythmic sound of the gloriously restored fountain filled the air. Carved marble horses reared majestically on their hind legs like they were fighting while streams of water shot straight up above their heads. Passing to the right of the fountain, she headed down the center of the driveway toward the main entrance. The grounds on either side were immaculate with incredible, towering oak trees overhead. She kept going until she could make out the massive, ornate wrought iron gates in the distance.

It would be so cool to get to come in that way. I wonder if there's one of those automatic gate opener thingies.

Spinning around, she retraced her steps and admired her professionally restored mansion.

It looks like it's brand new.

Working her way from top to bottom, Ana noticed the gleaming dark green tiles of the roof, the pressure-washed chimneys, dormers, trim, and every detail of the walls and windows on each level. The front veranda with those exquisite entrance doors was stunning. The visual tour didn't stop until she reached the dark, draped windows of Rudolph Griffin's study—the only room that hadn't been touched. Cleaning it was something she wanted to do all by herself.

I can't keep putting it off.

Skirting around the mansion and the garage, Ana didn't stop until she reached the rear terrace. She could instantly tell that everything had been cleaned. The stains, moss, rust, leaves and debris—all the evidence of years of neglect were completely gone.

Finally.

Stepping backwards, she took in the whole rear facade of the huge, private home. Every wall, window, door, and detail had been expertly pressure washed and restored. Turning around, Ana directed her gaze over the terrace at the extensive back lawn.

"Good night!" she gasped.

In the distance, the dazzling, white marble of the mausoleum glistened in the late afternoon sun. It literally almost took her breath away.

"Yes! Yes! Yes!" she cried.

The copper of the magnificent door, that for decades had been a dark, dingy green, now appeared to be on fire. Tears of joy filled her eyes as she made her way down the wide, marble terrace steps. In all of the commotion of Connor's party, she couldn't believe that she had not once looked in the direction of the mausoleum.

"This is how it's supposed to look!"

Ana thought about the Griffin family entombed inside, finally together again thanks to her dogged determination and inherited fortune. Suddenly, a slight movement caught her attention. Taking two steps to the right, she saw what it was and smiled.

It's Ricky.

Glancing over her shoulder to the left, Ana saw that the workers were all squatting on the ground and chatting with Andrew. At that moment he looked up and saw her. Ana waved at him, and he waved back

They must be taking a break.

Suddenly, the still inflated castle behind them lurched to the left. Ana shook her head.

Well, at least he's having a good time.

As she got closer to the ancient reptile, Ana could see that he was busy munching on the remains of the discarded floral arrangements from eight days before.

"You're just about out of flowers, aren't you?" She remarked as she got closer.

At the sound of her voice, Ricky stopped chewing and looked up. Ana walked over and stroked the top of his gnarled, 100+ year-old head. She watched as he went back to eating.

You know I love you, don't you?

Turning around, Ana leaned her back against the rough, shell. The slight up and down movement produced by the slow, rhythmic breathing of the enormous, gentle reptile caused her to remember.

Lewis loved you, too.

She recalled her promise to Rudolph Griffin, to take care of his dead son's exotic pet. Lifting her gaze to the left, Ana saw the corner of the mansion and thought about the massive metal door in the tunnel directly beneath it.

I'm glad Chuck and Andrew know.

Without warning, Ricky moved and threw her off balance. Ana glanced down at him. Then it hit her.

Oh, my goodness. I never showed them where I found you!

"See you later." Ana patted Ricky and took off jogging. She didn't stop until she rounded the corner of the mansion and came to the edge of the mowed lawn. She remembered that they had asked Johnson's Lawn Service not to touch the area surrounding the orchard. They never asked why.

I need to find the trap door.

Chapter Three

The tall, thick grass and weeds were higher than her knees. Concealed fallen branches and very nasty-looking briars forced Ana to choose her steps carefully. Without much trouble, she found the wide, steel grates in the ground that over the years had allowed ripened fruit to fall into the chamber below.

It ought to be about twenty feet from this one.

After pacing off the distance, Ana began searching the area. Several minutes later, she was still at it.

This is crazy! It's got to be right here!

While preparing for her twelfth birthday party back in January, Ana had gone outside to get something out of the car. As she closed the door, she had suddenly remembered that Ricky was still imprisoned in his underground room. Without anyone seeing her, Ana had made her way to the orchard, found the trap door, opened it, and freed the ancient tortoise. Now, however, in late spring, the ground was covered with thick grass and tangled weeds.

"Ugh," she fussed. "I'm getting nowhere fast."

Lifting her head, Ana tried to get her bearings. She gazed past the trees to the row of windows on the bottom floor of the mansion and then over to the closest steel grate.

I need to back up some.

When she did, she noticed a place where the grass and weeds had been matted down flat. A definite path tracked away in the direction of the mausoleum.

It looks like you-know-who has been here.

Ana walked to the middle of the spot and jumped up and down.

Thump. Thump. Thump.

A deep, hollow sound resonated beneath her feet.

"Bingo!"

Dropping to her knees, it took her only seconds to uncover the edges and locate the latch. Carefully, she inserted the two largest fingers of her right hand into the metal loop and pulled backwards.

Clunk!

The spring-loaded trap door popped open, but only slightly. Stringy, stubborn weeds held it in place. Positioning her hands along the edge, Ana pushed upwards on the lid until she could peer inside. Light poured in, revealing the wide ramp that sloped gradually downward into the underground chamber. Instinctively, Ana reached up and began cleaning the weeds off the top of the door but then stopped.

What am I doing? If I clean this off, then anybody will be able to find it.

Immediately, she thought about Lawrence Hill, the lawyer who had helped the Rudolph Griffin craft his will. After Griffin died, Hill spent years desperately searching the mansion trying to find it.

It's a miracle he never looked out here. There's no way he could have missed seeing this. He would have found Ricky and the tunnels and everything! Thank you, Lord!

Ana took a deep breath and let it out. Lowering the trap door back into place, she jumped on it until the latch snapped shut. A rustling noise to her right caused her to look up.

"Well, hello," she laughed. "Your ears must have been burning." Steadily crawling down the path, the giant tortoise headed straight for her. He was still munching on some of the withered roses. As he got closer Ana stepped backwards off the trap door. Ricky moved to where she had been standing and stopped. Lowering his head, he began nudging the edge of the door with his nose.

"Do you want to get back down into your palace?" Ricky lifted his old head, stared at her, and let out a series of low grunts and strange sounding squeaks.

"I'll take that as a yes," she chuckled.

Bending down to open the latch, she inserted her fingers into the loop like before. Just then, the faint sound of the large blower-vacuum from the other side of the mansion caused her to stop and stand back up. Ricky let out a couple of squeaks followed by a deep grunt and a long, definite hiss.

Ana could tell he was upset. "But, Sugar, I can't go off and just leave it open. Somebody might find it." The huge tortoise went back to bumping the trap door with its nose.

This is so sad!

"I'll talk to Andrew about it and see what we can do. I promise."

* * * * *

Conner and Andrew were standing next to each other and watching as the castle sank slowly to the ground. Ana crept up and stood silently behind them.

"Well, it's finally over," Connor sighed. "But all of my friends said that it was the best birthday party ever!"

"Your sister loves you."

"I know." Her little brother was quiet for several seconds. Ana knew his nine-year-old brain was churning. "Do you think she would buy me a blowup castle and set it up in our backyard?" Andrew sniffed and cleared his throat. She could tell her bodyguard was doing his best not to crack up. Finally, he rested his hand on Connor's shoulder.

"I seriously doubt it, pal."

* * * * *

Later in the Mercedes, as they followed the large truck toward the rear entrance of the estate, Ana noticed that Connor was being unusually quiet. She turned around so that she could see him. He was on his knees, staring out the rear window and mumbling. Ana strained to make out his words.

"Did you say something?"

"Thank you for my party," he uttered without turning around.

"You're welcome. I hope you had a good time?"

"I had a blast." He was still gazing out the rear window.

"I'm so glad."

For the next seven seconds the only audible sound was the humming of the car's engine.

"Ana?" The tone in his voice was different. She could tell he wanted something else.

"Yes, Connor."

He twisted around and stared at her. "Mom says that Mrs. Davis is finished cleaning the mansion, but that we're not going to move in and live there. She says you want us to stay in our old house. Is that right?"

"That's right."

"Why? It would be so cool! Why can't we live in your mansion?"

"I have my reasons." Ana hoped her response would end the matter. It didn't. Her brother squinted at her. She knew that look too.

"Well, if we're not going to live there, could me and my friends at least spend the night in it? You know, camp out in there? We were talking about it. It would be awesome! So, can we? Please? Please? Please?" His pleading mutated quickly into an irritating whine.

"No, Connor." She shook her head. Ana knew the best way to deal with him was to squash his crazy schemes as flat as a cockroach. "You can put that idea completely out of your head!"

Connor slumped in his seat. "I can't even think about it?"

"No, sir. You can't even think about it."

His request had caught her completely off guard. The thought of actually spending a night in her mansion had, oddly enough, never crossed her mind. But now, as they drove along, it was all she could think about.

Chapter Four

After dinner, as always, Ana helped her mother clean up the kitchen. Back in her bedroom, she picked up her Bible off the nightstand and sat down at her desk.

Her Sunday School teacher, Courtney Thompson, had told the girls, that if they would read the Bible passage and think about it before coming to class, that they would get so much more out of it. Ana remembered Olivia Freeman snorting and saying, "Well, that makes sense! Then we wouldn't sit here like a bunch of dummies when you ask us a question!" Ana had placed her bookmark in *The Gospel of Luke*, Chapter 19.

"Okay class." Ana tried to sound just like her teacher, whom she absolutely adored. "Here we go. Jesus visits Zacchaeus." After reading the story a couple of times, she closed her Bible, walked over, and crawled on top of her bed. For several minutes, Ana just lay there quietly, staring at the ceiling. She thought about her vast fortune.

Zacchaeus gave half of his money to poor people. Jesus didn't tell him that he had to do it. It was his idea! He wanted to do it.

She put her hands behind her head.

I ought to give half of my money to help poor people find good-paying jobs.

Ana grinned.

I can't wait to see the look on Chuck's face when I tell him. Oh no! That will mean that I've only got two-hundred million dollars left!

Rolling over, she gazed out the large bay window. The setting sun had turned the sky into gorgeous shades of blue and bright orange.

Lord, please let me know what I need to do.

A sudden, loud thud shook the whole house.

Leaping from her bed, Ana raced to the door and yanked it open. To her left, she could hear a stampede of heavy footsteps coming up the staircase. Her father leaped up the last two steps without stopping. Ana shook her head to let him know it wasn't her and pointed at her brother's door that was standing slightly open.

"Where's Mom?" asked Ana.

"She's in the shower!" Her father threw up his hands as he flew past and hurried toward Connor's room.

More heavy footsteps caused Ana to look back at the staircase. Andrew was only seconds behind her father. She had no idea her huge bodyguard could move so fast. His face looked like he had seen a ghost.

Holding her by the shoulders and checking her over from head to toe, he stammered, "Are you okay? Did you hurt yourself?"

"No. I'm fine. I think it was Connor."

"Praise the Lord," he exhaled but then looked embarrassed. "Wait. I didn't mean, Praise the Lord it's Connor, I meant…"

"I understand," she said and patted him on the arm. "Don't worry about it."

They quickly crossed the hall and entered her brother's room. Ana's father was on the floor holding him in his arms. Connor was rubbing the back of his head and moaning.

"Is he okay?"

"I think so."

"What on earth happened?"

"Well, judging from the chair over there on its side," Ana's father explained, motioning with his hand, "and the fact that his bed has been shoved against the wall. It looks like he tried to jump from the chair to the bed but didn't quite make it."

"Did it knock him out?" Andrew got down on his knees and gently touched Connor's shoulder. "Hey, Captain Apple Jacks. Okay, if I take a look at your eyes?" Ana's brother sniffed and turned toward her bodyguard without hesitation. Laying perfectly still, he let Andrew use his fingers to gently open and examine each eye.

This is amazing. He'll do anything for Andrew.

"Well, neither of his pupils look dilated, which is a good sign." Andrew moved his finger back and forth in front of his face. "Can you follow my finger with your eyes?" Connor did as instructed and stared back and forth. "Did it knock you out, pal?"

"I don't think so," Connor sniffed.

"He wasn't unconscious when I found him," explained Ana's father. "But he's got a serious bump on the back of his head. I think he maybe needs to be checked out."

"I'll go ahead and call 911," offered Andrew. Standing up, he whipped out his phone and punched in the numbers. He put it on speaker phone so that Ana's dad could listen in. After explaining what happened and giving the address, he said, "No. He's conscious, but he's got a large bump on the back of his head." The 911 operator assured that help was on the way. Andrew ended the call. "They'll more than likely want him to go to the hospital."

Connor at once stopped moaning and perked up. He stared at his father.

"Am I gonna get to ride in a' ambulance?"

"You might."

He sat up straight. "Can I call my friends and let 'em know I'm going to the hospital?

Ana's father shook his head. "No, it's too late."

"Will the ambulance go really fast? And turn on the flashing lights? And blow the siren?"

His father hugged him. "I hope not." Connor struggled free, stood up, and thrust out his hands.

"Why not?"

Andrew covered his mouth to hide a smile. Ana rolled her eyes and walked over next to him.

"He's fine," she muttered softly. "His head's as hard as a rock. We'd better check the floor and make sure it's okay."

Chapter Five

After examining Connor, the EMTs reported that he wasn't in any danger, but they did suggest taking him to the Emergency Room just to make sure. Connor, of course, was thrilled until he learned that there would be no trip in the speeding emergency vehicle with lights flashing and sirens blaring. Instead, his parents took him in the car.

Figuring that her little brother was not in great peril that demanded her presence, Ana retreated to her bedroom and closed the door. She sat down on the edge of her bed and said a prayer for her brother.

"Dear God, you know what a pain in the neck he is, but I don't ever want anything bad to happen to him. Please let his head be okay and forgive me for saying that he probably damaged the floor. Please be with Mom and Dad. And thank you that Andrew has such a calming effect on him."

For some unknown reason, praying for Connor reminded her of his request earlier in the day to spend the night in the mansion with his buddies. Ana fell backwards onto her bed and pursed her lips.

If I did spend the night, where would I sleep?

Other than the locked cellar, secret passageways, and Rudolph Griffin's study, which was still a mess, every inch of the mansion had been spotlessly cleaned.

Let's see...

Ana closed her eyes. In her mind, she began wandering around the first floor.

The rooms off the main hall won't do. The four guest rooms on the carpeted hall? No. I don't want my first night to be in one of them.

Still visualizing, she ascended the grand staircase to the second floor where nine stunningly beautiful guest suites awaited consideration. Ana grinned. She and her mother had had so much fun filming the documentary about the restoration of the mansion.

Any one of those would work.

She thought about Rudolph Griffin's imposing bedroom on the third floor. The dark-paneled walls. The gothic, cavern-like vaulted ceiling looming over her head. The lights from the brass chandeliers bathing the room in that warm, inviting, but masculine light. Oak logs blazing in the enormous stone fireplace at the far end of the room. Ana sighed but didn't open her eyes. She was enjoying the imaginary tour immensely.

The king-size, four-posted, dark mahogany bed on that lusciously thick Persian carpet commanding the center of the room. The fluffy, billowy pillows.

Oh, my! Look! The fabulous duvet bedcover and the insanely soft, pearl white sheets were turned down. The scene was complete. The bed was waiting on her to snuggle into its depths of delight. Oh, yes! Rudolph's Griffin's bedroom was a clear candidate for her first night in the mansion.

It would be absolutely amazing! But I probably wouldn't sleep a wink.

Back out on the third-floor balcony, she considered Lewis' bedroom but instantly vetoed that idea.

No. That wouldn't be right. Ever.

All at once Ana scrambled out of bed.

"Am I crazy?" she cried. "What am I doing?" Tears streamed out of her eyes. Seizing her head with her hands, Ana began stomping around the room, trying desperately to dislodge the image of Beatrice Griffin's death bed from her memory.

"How could I be this, this... stupid?"

Slumping in her desk chair, Ana tried to convince herself not to be afraid.

This is silly! Her room has been completely cleaned and sanitized! The bed linens and everything has been replaced with brand new stuff!

It was no use. As soon as she closed her eyes the disturbing images returned.

"Way to go, girl!" she fussed. Cupping her face with her hands, she said, "What am I going to do?" Spying her Bible on her desk again, she picked it up and held it against her chest.

What is that Psalm that Mom quotes whenever she's upset, or worried, or scared?

Cracking open her Bible in the middle, Psalm 19 stared her in the face.

Yes! Thank you, Jesus!

Feverishly, Ana read Psalm 19 but then stopped. "This isn't it." She glanced at the next Psalm. "Uh...? Nope." Psalm 21. "Uh...? Nope." Ana sighed and read the first few lines of Psalm 22. "Nope." Psalm 23. "Wait a minute— The Lord is my Shepherd I shall not want. Bingo! Yes! This is it!" she cried. Ana kept reading out loud: "He makes me lie down in green pastures. He leads me beside still waters. He restores my soul."

Wow! This is really good! Thank you, God!

Ana felt her nerves calming down. She kept reading until she came to the part that read, "You prepare a table before me in the presence of my enemies." That reminded her of eating in the school lunchroom under the evil stares of Skylar Perkins and her gang.

Skylar's not really my enemy, not anymore. She's just got a super bossy personality.

Without warning, another possible enemy came to mind.

Lawrence Hill. Even though he's a lawyer, he would still probably like to strangle me if he had the chance. It's a good thing that Andrew and the police have his fingerprints.

Ana read the last verse of the Psalm: "Surely goodness and mercy will follow me all the days of my life. And I will dwell in the house of the Lord, forever." As she closed her Bible, a light clicked on in her head.

House of the Lord?

"That's it!" she howled. "I don't have to sleep in the mansion by myself! I can invite my Sunday School class. We could have a slumber party!"

After getting dressed for bed and still thinking about her great idea, Ana grabbed her pile of dirty clothes and headed across the hall to the bathroom.

I can ask Mrs. Thompson tomorrow and find out what she thinks.

Tossing the clothes into the hamper, Ana was almost back in her room when she slammed on the brakes.

"Oops!"

Returning to the bathroom, she yanked her jeans out of the hamper and checked the back pocket. Carefully, she removed the small white envelope. Back in her bedroom, Ana carefully pulled out the card. She studied the odd drawing again.

I know I've seen this some place before.

Suddenly, an extremely pleasant thought crossed her mind.

I'll show it to Carter in church tomorrow. Maybe he can help me figure it out.

Ana picked up her Bible and opened it to Psalm 23. After inserting the card back into the envelope, she placed it into the Bible and shut it.

This way I won't forget it.

In bed, she reached up to turn off the lamp on her nightstand but then didn't.

Maybe I'll just leave it on tonight.

Ana turned over and closed her eyes. Twenty minutes later she was still wide awake. She tried covering her head with her pillow, but that didn't work either.

Like a leaf caught by the wind, her recent memories darted back and forth: from Ricky and the trap door in the orchard, to Connor's accident, to inviting her class to her slumber party, to Beatrice's bedroom and the fact that it was now all cleaned up, to Psalm 23, to Griffin's card with the odd drawing, and finally, to showing it to Carter tomorrow in church.

Removing her pillow, Ana turned over, reached up, and clicked off the light. In the darkness, she closed her eyes, sighed deeply, and grinned.

Carter Hudson.

Chapter Six

Sunday morning, Ana was waiting on the bottom step of the stairs, already dressed for church when Andrew came ambling down the hall. He was clearly not ready to leave. She sprang to her feet to face him.

"Now, why do I get the feeling that this is not going to be a normal Sunday morning?" he muttered.

"I need us to get to church a little earlier today if you don't mind. I want to ask my teacher something."

"Do I have time for a cup of coffee and a bite of breakfast?"

"Of course." Anna turned and led the way to the kitchen. "I just wanted you to know."

Her father was already sitting at the table and cradling his half-full cup of coffee. He glanced up as she and Andrew walked in.

"Good morning," they said in unison.

"Good morning to you." He opened his eyes wide and shook his head at Ana. "Wow. You're already dressed. What's up?"

"If it's okay with you and Mom, I want to get to church a little earlier today."

"It's fine with me." Her father picked up his toast to take another bite. Ana looked around the room.

"Where's Mom?"

"Upstairs with your brother. He's having Apple Jacks in bed this morning. She said he had a rough night last night. I think he's feeling the results of his crash."

"Is he okay?" asked Andrew.

"Just sore. With a big bruise on his rear end. But at least the bump on the back of his head has gone down."

"I'll be right back." Ana scurried out the door, down the hall, and up the stairs. When she entered Connor's room, her mother turned toward her and put her finger to her lips. Her little brother was sound asleep.

"I need to ask you something," whispered Ana into her ear. Her mother motioned toward the door. Ana followed her out into the hall.

"Mom, is it okay if I have a slumber party in the mansion and invite the girls from my Sunday School class?"

"Oh, that sounds like a lot of fun." Ana could tell she was excited about the idea. "We didn't get the place all cleaned up for nothing, right? When do you want to have it?"

"I don't know yet. I've asked Andrew to take me a little earlier this morning, so I can discuss it with Mrs. Thompson before asking the girls. But I first wanted to get your permission."

Nancy smiled sweetly. "I think a slumber party is a wonderful idea. Let me know how I can help."

Ana hugged her around the neck. "Thanks, Mom. You're the best."

Back in the kitchen, Ana fixed herself two pieces of toast and sat down next to her father.

"So, what's this all about?" he asked. Ana explained her reasons for wanting to leave a little earlier than usual. "Do you mind if I ride with you? Your mother's staying with Connor, so there's no need for the three of us to take two cars."

"Would you like to drive the Mercedes?" offered Andrew. Ronnie Stilwell held up his hand.

"I appreciate the offer, but I don't want to have to answer all the questions, as to why I'm driving Miss Ana Stilwell to church instead of you." There was an odd look on her father's face.

"Oh, I completely understand." Andrew chuckled. "There's no need to stir that pot."

"Pot? What pot?" Ana held up her hands. "What are you two talking about?"

Her father was about to take another sip of coffee but stopped and held his cup in mid-air. "Honey, I'm sure life in Lewistowne was pretty dull before you became so...well, before you became the talk of the town."

She looked at Andrew. He nodded in agreement.

"People watch every move you make," he said.

* * * * *

Later that morning, Ana stared out the window as Andrew made the right turn onto Church Street.

"I wish you hadn't told me," she muttered.

"Told you what?" he asked.

"That people are constantly watching me. That's just creepy."

"It comes with the territory, young lady," her father said as they turned into the church parking lot. "Fame has its price."

On their way to the education building, Ana, Andrew, and her father had to wait at the curb for a car to pass. The woman in the front seat grabbed the arm of her husband who was driving and excitedly pointed across him in Ana's direction. The man jerked around, stared at Ana, and flashed her a toothy grin. Behind them, a girl maybe Connor's age pressed her nose against the window. Her eyes and mouth were wide open.

Ana glanced up at her father and Andrew. They both acted like they hadn't noticed the family. Inside the building, her father broke the silence: "See you two in worship." He lightly touched Ana on the shoulder. "Hang in there, Tiger. Don't let it get to you." He disappeared through a door that led to a nearby stairwell.

Farther down the hall, Ana noticed two older men standing in the welcome area, drinking coffee, and talking to each other. As she and Andrew got closer, one of the men motioned with his head in their direction. The other man turned around and stared at her. Ana sighed.

Okay. Let's see if I can nip this in the bud.

Ana marched up and stuck out her hand. "Good morning, gentlemen!"

I've seen them somewhere before.

"Oh, uh! Good morning, Miss Stilwell." The shorter of the two men fumbled with his cup and moved it quickly to his left hand.

"I'm Bob Matthews." He gently shook her fingers. "It is nice to finally meet you." His whole upper body moved slightly forward.

Did he just bow?

The other man had already set down his cup on a nearby table and now stood at attention like he was waiting on his turn to greet the Queen of England. When Ana extended her hand, he graciously took it in his.

"Good morning, Miss Stilwell." His voice broke as he spoke. "I'm Alan Arden." Ana was surprised when he, too, slightly bowed.

This is crazy! Why are they acting like this?

Suddenly, she remembered where she had seen them before.

They take up the offering in the worship service. They must know how much money I give. This is embarrassing.

"Oh, please. Just call me, Ana." The two men smiled but didn't say anything. "I hope you have a nice Sunday." She and Andrew continued down the hall. When they were far enough away to not be overheard, he leaned down toward her.

"Smart move, Chief. That should make them start treating you like a normal, little girl."

"Leave me alone."

At the door to her classroom, Andrew offered, "You want me to wait out here until you finish talking to your teacher?"

"No. I'll be fine. I'll see you later after Sunday School." She watched as he made his way back down the hall. Her teacher was already in the classroom with her head down as she tapped on her cellphone. Ana waited in the doorway.

"Oh, good morning," Courtney Thompson glanced up briefly in Ana's direction. "Just a moment. I'm almost finished." Seconds later, she placed her phone onto the table and smiled. "So, what brings you here so early on this fine Sunday morning?"

Ana walked into the room. "I've got an idea, and I wanted to know what you think about it before I say anything to the other girls."

"Well, I'm all ears." Ana's teacher sat down and motioned at the chair to her left. "Come over here and have a seat." Her kind manner put Ana at once at ease.

"I would like to invite the girls and you to a slumber party in my mansion." Ana saw the astonishment on her teacher's face.

"Are you serious? That would be...amazing! Are you sure you want me to come, too?"

"Of course!" Ana gestured with her hands. "You're our teacher."

Ana stood up and paced back and forth. "I thought we could eat in the main dining hall and then have our meetings in one of the parlors on the first floor." She stopped and glanced over at Mrs. Thompson. "We can all sleep on the second floor. There are nine guest rooms. Each one has two queen-size beds and its own private bathroom. We could put two girls in a room."

"That sounds perfect."

"Of course, we'll have to work out who sleeps where."

"Leave that up to me," said Mrs. Thompson. "We'll draw names out of a hat or something."

"That would work." Ana held up her left hand and using her right index finger acted like she was checking off items on a list. "Everyone could arrive at 6 p.m. on Friday, check into their rooms, and get unpacked. Then we'll eat dinner, have our meeting in the largest parlor, have fun, and play games until midnight. Then we'll go to sleep, get up on Saturday, eat breakfast, have a meeting, go for a morning swim, get dressed, pack up, and then leave before lunch."

"Wow! You've given this a lot of thought."

Ana nodded. "I'll take care of everything." She returned to pointing at her fingers. "The girls will need to bring pajamas, a change of clothes, a swimsuit for Saturday, their toothbrush, and...," Ana paused. "Oh yeah, a pair of soft house shoes because of the floors."

"Right," Mrs. Thompson made notes on a piece of paper she had taken out of her Bible. Ana watched her.

"Oh yes!" she added, "Each girl needs to be sure and bring her Bible. That'll be the best part." Ana held up her hand like she was ready to testify. "We will finally, finally have enough time to talk!"

Mrs. Thompson chuckled, "Oh, yes. You girls definitely need more time to talk." Ana moved closer to her teacher who was still seated in her chair making notes.

"Can you think of anything else?"

"Uh," her teacher smiled and put down her pen. "If it's not too much trouble, would it be possible for us to take a tour of the whole mansion? I would love to see everything." Ana stepped backwards.

The whole mansion? Everything?

The request had caught her totally off guard.

"Is there something wrong?" Her teacher took her by the hand. "Are you okay?"

"Oh, sure." Ana managed a weak smile. "I can show you around." Her mind raced from one incredible or unnerving secret to the next.

"Oh, this is so exciting," cooed her teacher. Ana swallowed and nodded.

Oh, it'll be exciting all right.

Chapter Seven

"May I be excused?" Ana asked her teacher as she backed toward the classroom door. "I need a drink of water."

"Oh, sure," said Mrs. Thompson. "There's plenty of time before class starts. In fact, I think I'll go get a cup of coffee."

When Ana reached the water fountain, there was already a line of people waiting. Directly in front of her was a very tall, middle-aged lady wearing a light green dress. There were tiny, yellow butterflies all over it. Next was a much older, heavier woman and then two giggling, wiggling girls. Ana leaned out to see who was first in line and sighed.

He looks to be about the same age as Connor.

Ana watched as the boy pressed the button on and off, causing little, broken streams of water to arc through the air.

Great. He even acts like Connor.

The tall lady in front of Ana loudly cleared her throat several times. The boy playing with the fountain did not get the hint. Ana noticed that the halls were filling with people making their way to their respective classes. Out of the corner of her eye, she could tell that every adult who passed by was staring at her.

I wish Dad and Andrew had never told me.

Turning back around, she figured the tall woman in front of her had been watching her, too, because all the butterflies on her dress were fluttering back into place.

Good grief.

The boy finished, and the line moved forward.

"What's up, rich girl?"

Ana whirled around and stared into the grinning face of Carter Hudson.

"That does it! Nobody is this thirsty!" She shot him a look, pushed past him, and hurried down the hall.

"Hey!" he called and ran to catch up with her. "What's eating you?" Ana halted in her tracks and turned to face him.

"Do you know what it's like having everyone constantly stare at you? Watch every move *you* make?" Trying to hide his amusement, Carter immediately clamped his hand over his mouth. It didn't help.

Laughing, he blurted out, "Uh, no!" and leaned in closer to her. "But, then again, I'm not insanely rich like you are. If I was, I'm sure people would stare a hole through me, too."

"Well, I am so tired of it!" she grumbled. "I wish I could go back to being normal again."

"Really?" Several people stopped and began watching them. Carter grabbed her tenderly by the shoulders and pulled her closer to him. "What would happen to all those people you're helping? You know—the ones with cancer. And what about the military families?" Ana gazed into his perfect blue eyes.

"I know. I know," she said and let out a deep sigh. "I guess you're right."

"Of course, I'm right." Straining to hear, an older couple inched closer to them. Carter turned and shot them a cheesy grin. "Oops! Show's over. Y'all have a nice Sunday." He escorted Ana across the hall into an empty classroom. She gladly let him.

"It's just..." she started again, but Carter interrupted her.

"It's just nothing. Come on. Snap out of it." His nose was almost touching hers. "For crying out loud. You're Ana Stilwell!" He stepped backwards and held out his arms toward her. "Ana Stilwell. You're the most famous person in the whole town and probably the richest kid in the whole state...maybe in the whole world!"

Ana just stood there. She could tell he wasn't finished, but she loved the sound of his voice.

"You've got a fabulous mansion and a huge estate with tennis courts and your very own swimming pool. You own the town's newspaper and lots of other companies. You've got millions of shares of stock." Ana watched him take a breath and gather more steam. "You own property in Europe that you've never even seen." He paused and Ana could tell he was trying to think. "You've got two Mercedes!" He held up two fingers, "Two! And a BMW, and who knows what else."

Ana snickered. "There's an old motorcycle that's supposed to be very rare and very valuable," she added.

"Really?" He bugged out his eyes. Ana nodded.

"It's in the garage." She held up her finger. "Oh, yeah, I also own a huge yacht that I've never seen. It's somewhere in Italy."

"Exactly!" he cried. "While other kids our age were doodling around here on spring break, we flew to Vienna, Austria and stayed in a fabulous hotel. What an adventure! You found Mr. Griffin, alive, in that castle..." Immediately, Ana held up her finger and pressed it against his mouth, effectively shushing him.

"Shh! Thank you. That's enough!" she whispered. Slowly removing her finger, she pressed it against her own lips. "We don't talk about that. Ever." Carter blushed and then broke into a wide grin.

"If you say so."

"I say so." Instantly, Ana thought about the mysterious message from Rudolph Griffin that she wanted to show him, but then remembered it was still in her Bible, lying on the table in her Sunday School class.

"Rats," she muttered.

"Rats? What wrong, now?"

"Before he died, you-know-who left me a mysterious message. He wrote it on a small card that Chuck found in the envelope with the new will."

"Are you serious?" Carter's eyes almost popped out of his head. "That is wild. May I see it?"

"It's in my Bible in my Sunday School class! I'll show it to you after worship service."

"Can't," he replied, shaking his head. "We're heading out of town and won't be back until late tonight. Just wait and show it to me tomorrow in school during lunch."

"Sounds like a plan," she grinned.

The first gong calling everyone to Sunday School sounded. "Come on," said Carter. "We don't need to be late to our classes."

As she floated down the hall, the constant stares of those passing by didn't bother her. Not anymore. In her mind, she was back standing on that amazing medieval balcony with Carter Hudson. Another gong echoed through the hall as she entered the room.

Ana froze in her tracks.

Mrs. Thompson was at the far end, and all of her classmates were seated where they usually were. Ana's chair on the other side of the table was empty like she expected it to be. Seated directly in front of her, however, was a new girl. Her back was to Ana, but Ana didn't need to see her face. All that shocking red hair was a dead give-away.

It's Skylar Perkins!

Chapter Eight

Ana kept her head down as she moved around to the right and made her way to her seat.

What is she doing here? Now, if I invite everyone to my slumber party, I'll have to invite her, too. This is a disaster.

"Girls." Every head turned towards Mrs. Thompson. Ana's teacher smiled and gestured to the opposite end of the table. "Please let me introduce our newest class member. This is Skylar Perkins." All heads rotated in the opposite direction. All, that is, except Ana's. Her gaze stopped on Olivia Freeman, sitting directly across from her. Ana grinned because Olivia was glaring at the new girl.

Oh, good. Maybe she'll make some crack about Skylar's hair or something. What if Skylar gets upset and just leaves?

Almost as soon as she thought it, Ana felt bad for secretly wanting such a thing in the first place. She lowered her head and prayed without closing her eyes.

Lord, please, forgive me. I don't need to act like this, just because Skylar can be so... difficult.

Mrs. Thompson continued, "Skylar, would you like to tell us a little about yourself?"

"Well," Skylar glanced around the room, "there's not much to tell." Something about the tone in her voice made Ana's head pop up. "I was born in Lewistowne. I've lived here all my life and I go to the same school as Ana." She gestured toward Ana with her head. "Several weeks ago, we started coming to worship here." Her voice quivered. "Pastor Barnes talked with my mom and dad. He said that we ought to attend Sunday School, too. So, here I am."

This is unreal.

Stunned, Ana cautiously studied the expression on Skylar's face, hoping to detect some clue for the obvious transformation.

Either she is the greatest actor in the world, or something has happened to her!

"Well, we are very glad to have you here with us today." Ana's teacher shifted in her chair to the left. "And now, before we begin our Bible study this morning, Ana has a special announcement to make." She motioned with her hand. "Ana?"

What do I do? I can't back out now.

Swallowing hard, Ana pushed back her chair and slowly stood up. All the excitement about inviting everyone to her first ever slumber party was gone, replaced with a mixture of panic and dread. Turning to her teacher, Ana managed a weak but very fake smile.

"I, uh, would like to invite you, uh, all to a slumber party in my mansion." Ana gazed around the table. Every single mouth was gaping wide open. Even Skylar Perkins'.

"Are you kidding me?" shouted Olivia. "Oh, wow! I can't believe it! I can't wait to tell my mom. All she talks about is you and your money and your enormous mansion! This is going to be so cool!" Every head bobbed up and down in agreement. "When? When do you want us to come?"

Ana glanced at her teacher. Her head was bobbing up and down, too.

"Well, I was thinking maybe a Friday night..."

"Friday night?" exploded Olivia. "This Friday night? Really? Oh, wow! Wow! Wow!" Several of the girls began clapping and enthusiastically nodding.

"Well, I don't know if Ana meant this coming Friday night." Courtney Thompson held up her hand and shot Ana a surprised but hopeful look. Ana managed another grin in return.

"Sure. This Friday will be fine. It only gives me a week to get ready, but I've got people who can help me."

The girls began clapping and Ana's teacher held up her hands. "But first, each of you will need to check with your parents. Ask them to please text me this afternoon, if you are coming, so I can let Ana know."

Ana watched as Olivia jumped up and waved at the other girls. "Can you believe it? We're going to get to spend the night in Ana Stilwell's mansion—this coming Friday night!"

"If you get your parents' permission," reminded Mrs. Thompson. "Let them know that I will be there, too. Along with other adults that will be helping with the evening." She smiled at Ana.

"Permission?" cackled Olivia. "My mom's gonna' freak flat out! She'll want to come, too! But no parents allowed! Right?"

The room erupted with the lively chatter of very excited twelve-year old girls. Courtney Thompson let them enjoy the moment. Out of the corner of her eye, Ana noticed that Skylar was acting like...well, not like Skylar Perkins.

What is going on here?

Thinking back, Ana recalled how *the queen of the sixth grade* had made her life miserable from her first day of school. Then after she found Rudolph Griffin's lost will and became so wealthy, Ana remembered the day when Skylar begged her for help, because her dad had lost his job. Ana had felt sorry for her and got him a nice-paying position at her newspaper. Skylar had seemed so thankful, at least, back then. But it didn't take long for her and her gang to begin spreading rumors again. They were all crazy about Carter Hudson and were jealous that he had paid so much attention to Ana, even before she had become so famous.

When Mrs. Thompson announced the Scripture passage, Ana watched Skylar flipping back and forth in the front half of her Bible.

Luke is in the New Testament, not the Old.

Then she noticed that most of the pages were sticking together.

That's a brand-new Bible!

Maggie Benson, who was sitting next to Skylar, must have noticed that she was having trouble finding the text. She whispered something. Skylar nodded and handed her the Bible. After easily finding Luke, Chapter 19, Maggie gave it back to her and patted her on the hand.

The teacher began by briefly telling the story of Jesus and Zacchaeus and then read the passage in the Bible. "Okay," she asked, "What did you learn about Jesus?" Each girl responded. Ana could tell that they enjoyed studying God's Word like this. When it was Skylar's turn, Ana, dying to know what she was going to say, listened carefully.

"Jesus was nice to Zac..., uh, to that man."

"Zacchaeus," said Mrs. Thompson, coming to her rescue.

Skylar repeated slowly: "Zac-chae-us,".

Ana stared at her. All the aggravation and just plain old suffering that Skylar had caused her in the past for some reason just melted away.

Later during the worship service, Ana sat between Andrew and her father, but kept glancing over at Skylar who was sitting with her parents.

The pastor, Dr. Barnes, was preaching on the same passage they had studied in Sunday School.

"Zacchaeus' whole life changed after he got to know Jesus and became one of His followers," he explained.

Ana closed her eyes and prayed for Skylar.

Chapter Nine

As they drove out of the church parking lot, Ana's father spoke up from the back seat.

"Oh, yes. I almost forgot. We need to run by *Tasty Chicken*. Your mother asked me to bring home lunch."

"Don't forget to order extra biscuits with lots of honey for Master Stilwell," added Andrew.

"And for you!" teased Ana.

Minutes later, Andrew guided the Mercedes into the narrow drive thru of Lewistowne's much beloved fast-food establishment. There were several well-known, fast-food restaurants out on the by-pass, but they could not match this place. At least seven cars were in line ahead of them.

"It is worth the wait," said her father. Ten minutes later several large, plain, bulging paper bags graced the back seat. As they drove along, the tantalizing aroma wafted through the luxury vehicle. Suddenly, Andrew's stomach growled loud enough for Ana hear it.

"What was that?" Twisting her head around, she acted like she was looking for evidence out the rear window. "Did we run over something?" Her dad burst out laughing. Just then, his stomach let out a long, deep gurgle, too.

"Wow!" she snickered. "We better get home quick before you two explode!"

"Amen to that," exclaimed Andrew. He pressed on the gas pedal and increased the speed. Seconds later, Ana began moving her head back and forth, as she stared out the windows. He glanced over at her. "What are you doing?"

"Watching out for the police."

* * * * *

As they walked through the front door, Ana got her father's attention. "I'm going up to check on Mom and Connor."

"Good idea. Please, tell her we brought lunch."

"Yes, sir."

Connor's door was open. Ana peeked in and saw her mother sitting in a chair and reading one of her *Magnolia* magazines.

"We're back," she whispered. Her brother was not in his bed. "Where is he?"

"In the tub." Her mother motioned with her head. "I completely forgot to make him take a bath after his party yesterday. Then in all the commotion last night when he fell, I, well, I didn't think about it. But this morning when the smell became unbearable..." Nancy Stilwell lowered her magazine and sighed. "I don't think he's had a bath since last Thursday."

Ana laughed, "He would never take a bath if you didn't make him."

"I know. I know," her mother looked up. "Did your father get lunch?"

"Yes, ma'am."

"That's good." She stood up, waving her arms. "Please, help me move your brother's bed back in place." She grabbed the footboard and Ana moved to the headboard that had been jammed against the wall. Connor's bed was made of solid wood. Bracing herself against the dark, wainscot paneling on the wall, Ana pushed.

"That's good," said her mother. She walked out into the hall and turned toward the bathroom. "Connor!" she called. "It's time to get out."

"But I'm not ready!"

Ana shook her head.

He fusses when he has to take a bath and then he fusses when he has to get out.

She turned and looked at the wall to see if the bed had damaged it.

Huh?

Along the inside right edge of the flat, framed panel, Ana noticed a dark, narrow slit.

The wood must have shifted when his bed hit it.

There was just enough room between the headboard and the wall for her to bend down and get a closer look. Placing her hands flat onto the panel, Ana pushed to the right. The flat piece of wood slid easily back into place.

Click.

The metallic sound was so soft that she almost didn't hear it. Almost.

Well, that's not normal.

Placing her hands back on the panel, she pushed it to the left.

Click.

It opened easily to reveal a hollow, dark space behind it.

"It's a hidden compartment!" she squealed but then hushed herself.

"Connor get out of the tub this instant!" Her mother's voice commanded from down the hall. "Your father brought home *Tasty Chicken* and Andrew is going to eat up all the biscuits if you don't hurry up and get a move on!"

"Oh, no!" yelled her little brother. The sound of tub water sloshing let Ana know she had run out of time.

Uh, oh.

"I need a towel!" he yelled.

"I'm getting you one!"

Ana slid the panel back into place, stood up, and scooted out of the room. She made it to her bedroom and shut the door just seconds before Connor ran out of the bathroom, fussing, and struggling to keep himself covered with the large, white towel.

Listening quietly at her door, Ana could hear her mother cleaning up her brother's mess on the bathroom floor. The last of the tub water gurgled down the drain, as Connor—now completely dressed—bolted from his room.

"Connor, dear, please be careful!" her mother called as she followed him down the stairs. Ana stepped out into the hall and started in the direction of her brother's room, but then stopped.

Flashlight.

Spinning around, she went straight to her dresser and pulled open the second drawer from the top. Ana grinned. Her flashlight was right where she had left it, buried beneath her underwear. As she gazed at the slender object in her right hand, a cascade of memories, some thrilling and others terrifying, washed over her.

We've been through a lot together, haven't we?

The spine-tingling sensation that she had felt so many times before was back. She clicked the switch on and off just to make sure the batteries were still good. Like a cat, Ana slinked toward the open door of Connor's bedroom.

I can't wait to see what's in there.

"Ana!" called her father from downstairs. She jumped like she had been shot.

"Yes, sir?" she answered, calmly and respectfully, not wanting to let on that she was up to something much more exciting than eating *Tasty Chicken* with the family.

"Come on, honey! Let's eat!"

Ana rolled her eyes. "Be right there!"

* * * * *

After lunch, Connor went at once to his room and shut the door. Any thoughts of exploring the mysterious hidden compartment would have to wait. Ana ambled into the living room and plopped down in the chair that she usually sat in for their family movie night.

I have millions of dollars. I can get almost anything I want. But all I want right now is to know what's behind that panel!

"What's wrong? Are you bored?"

Ignoring Andrew's question for a moment, Ana kept staring out the window. She wasn't bored, just frustrated. Ana sighed and turned to face him.

"No. Just thinking."

"About your spend-the-night party?"

"It's a 'slumber party'. And how do you know about that?"

"Your mom mentioned it to your dad while she was setting the table."

"What was his reaction?"

"Interesting."

"What's that mean?"

Andrew chuckled. "I think he's sad that he's not a member of your Sunday School class."

"That's funny." Ana went back to staring out the window. After a moment, she glanced over at Andrew who was still standing. "Want to drive me over to the mansion?"

"I have a better idea." His hands were on his hips. "Why don't we walk?"

She laughed. "Walk? You? Walk?"

"Okay, hike." Andrew held out his hands. "Why don't we hike down the creek and you show me how you get into the mansion."

Ana stood up. "Why it that so important?"

"If you found it, then somebody else could find it, too. They could get into the mansion just like you did," he explained.

"Okay. Okay," she huffed as she walked past him. "I need to go change my clothes." Ana motioned at him with her head. "And you might want to change into some old clothes, too." He was still wearing his nice Sunday jeans and a white shirt.

"Why?" Andrew stroked the front of his shirt with his hands. "Are you afraid I'll fall in?"

Ana wagged her head. "You, making it down the creek is not the problem. You, making it through the small opening in the boulder, that's the problem."

63

Chapter Ten

"You know, this is actually a lot of fun," Andrew called as he followed Ana as they jumped from rock to rock.

"I'm *so glad* you're having a good time," she kidded without looking back at him.

When they reached the most treacherous spot in the journey, Ana didn't hesitate. She crossed the stream, hopping back and forth like a pro.

"You're joking, right?" Andrew rubbed his chin. Ana laughed and re-crossed the stream stepping and leaping from side to side without stopping until she was standing beside him.

"Now, just watch me and do exactly what I do." Andrew nervously watched her every move until she reached the other side.

"That's easy for you to say."

"You were the one who insisted we do this." She gestured back up the creek. "If you want to go home that's fine, with me!"

"No. No. I'm coming." Stretching his arms out wide, Ana's huge bodyguard began tiptoeing and leaping across the rocks.

"You look like a giant ballerina!" she laughed.

Andrew stopped to catch his breath and glanced up. "Have I ever told you that you can be a real pain in the neck?"

"Several times."

After two more jumps, he reached the bank.

"Bravo!" she clapped. "Now, that wasn't so bad, was it?" She pulled out her cell phone to check the time.

"Oh, wow. Is that the wall to the estate?"

Ana turned to see where he was pointing.

"Yep. That's it."

They didn't stop again until they reached the sandbar directly across the creek from the huge boulder beneath the stone wall.

After catching his breath, Andrew asked, "So, what do we do now?"

"The hidden entrance is directly in front of us. Can you see it?" The tone in her voice had an almost irritated ring to it. Andrew walked to the edge of the water and systematically searched the opposite bank. After a couple of minutes, he shook his head.

"I don't see it. How did you ever find it?"

"God showed me where it was."

"Oh, yeah," he laughed. "I forgot."

Crossing over to the other side, Ana made her way down the bank to the huge boulder. Andrew was right behind her.

"Wait here," she instructed. Hugging the face of the massive rock, Ana stepped onto the narrow, submerged ledge at the base and worked her way across the surface. When she got to the crevice, she inserted her fingers, found the lever, and pressed down on it.

Clunk.

The perfectly concealed door in the rock popped open.

"This is incredible!" Andrew cried and moved closer. "How did you figure all of this out?"

She rolled her eyes at him, pushed open the door, crawled through the opening, turned around, and poked her head back out.

"Come on. Just be careful."

Andrew inched down the boulder until he could see inside. She watched as he examined the opening.

"So, what do you think? Pretty tight fit, huh?"

"I have to be honest." He wasn't smiling. "It's going to be a very tight fit."

"Well, you were the one who insisted on doing this, so come on," she said as she backed away from the door. Above her head in the wall to her right, Ana saw the narrow crevice with the other door lever. "Hey, wait a minute."

"What is it now?"

"There's another lever in here that, I hope, opens the door from inside. I need to know if it works."

"Do we have to do it now?"

"Yes!" she stared at him. "I've never had a chance to do this. It won't take but a minute." Ana inched her way deeper into the tunnel as she spoke. "Okay. Now shut the door. I'll try to open it from in here. If it doesn't open, just stick your fingers in the hole out there, push the lever down, and it will pop back open."

"Are you sure about this?"

"Yes. I'm sure."

"Okay." Leaning to the side, Andrew slowly closed the thick granite door.

Clunk.

Instantly, the secret tunnel was plunged into total darkness. As she fumbled for her flashlight, a familiar chill snaked its way down Ana's back. She remembered how terrified she was the first time she had explored the tunnel and feared that she had been sealed inside.

"Are you okay?" Andrew's muffled voice from the other side was barely audible, but it had an instant, calming effect on Ana's nerves.

"I'm fine," she yelled. There was no light seeping in at all, not even through the seams around the edge of the door.

This is wild!

Clicking on her flashlight, Ana examined the inside of the door. Twisting around, she reached up, inserted her fingers into the hole, found the lever, and pulled down on it.

Clunk.

"I'm glad that's over," Andrew muttered as he pushed open the door. Ana expected a relieved look on his face, but instead she could tell that he was in the process of changing his mind about squeezing through the tiny portal.

"I really appreciate your help," she grinned. "Okay. Are you ready? Think thin!"

"You know." He felt the sides of the tunnel and shook his head. "On second thought, there's really no need for me to even try."

"There's not?"

"No, not really," he said leaning backwards. "First of all, this door is almost impossible to see from out here, and second, all we need to do is put some cement in this hole with the lever, just to be safe."

"Well, that's not happening," she frowned.

"Why not?"

"Because I don't want it to." She stared at him and waved her hand. "Please move so I can get out." Andrew backed away from the opening back along the edge of the huge boulder. Ana crawled out and shut the door behind her. "We'll just have to think of some other way to keep people from finding it."

"Does it really mean that much to you?"

"Yes. It means that much to me." She wiped her hands on her jeans and started back up the creek. "It was Lewis Griffin's idea to dig this tunnel and to build this secret door." She turned around and glared at her large bodyguard. "So, I don't want it changed in any way...ever."

"Yes, ma'am," he saluted.

Neither of them said another word for at least five minutes. Finally, Andrew broke the silence.

"You know what?"

"What?"

"If you could buy the two houses next to yours. He waved his hand in the air. "You would own all the land that borders the creek." Ana halted and stared at him.

"You know, that is not a bad idea. I'll ask Chuck to work on it."

"But what if the owners won't sell?"

"Oh, I think they will." She grinned at him. "I'll just make them an offer they won't refuse."

* * * * *

When they reached the most difficult crossing again, Ana went first. On the other side, she quickly pulled out her cell phone and held it up in front of her face.

"Come on, twinkle toes," she called. Half-way across, Andrew put his left foot on the edge of a large flat stone, instead of in the center. Without warning, the rock tilted downward under his weight. "Careful!" she shouted, but it was too late.

"Oh! Ah! No!"

Ana watched as he wobbled and struggled to regain his balance. It was no use.

Ker-splash!

Standing knee-deep in the stream, he hollered, "This water is freezing!"

"Oh, don't I know it!" she howled and pointed at her phone. "And the best part is, I got it all right here!"

Sloshing up onto the bank, Andrew stomped his feet. "So, what's it going to take for you to delete that little episode?"

"Oh, I'm keeping this one." She laughed. "You never know when I might need it."

* * * * *

Connor was sitting on the porch steps as they emerged into the back yard.

"What happened to you?" he hooted and pointed at Andrew's, soaked pants. "Did you fall in?"

Andrew didn't respond to Connor's taunt but instead held up a small, quartz stone he had dug out of his right shoe. "I got this from the creek," he called. "It looks like it might have gold in it!"

"Are you serious?" Connor leaped off the steps and raced toward them. "Let me see it! Let me see it!"

Andrew handed him the rock. Ana's brother held it up to the sunlight.

"Where did you see gold?"

"Right there." Andrew pointed at a brown dot. "Doesn't that look like gold?" Connor picked at the spot until the tiny speck came loose.

"It's just a piece of sand!"

"Are you sure?"

"Yes, I'm sure!" He threw the worthless rock into the bushes and stomped away.

"Well, at least, he's not making fun of my wet clothes anymore," said Andrew.

Ana didn't respond. As she watched Connor climb the steps up to their back porch, all she could think about was the hidden space behind the paneled wall in his bedroom.

I'll need to wait until he's asleep.

Chapter Eleven

It was 11:37 p.m. when Ana deftly pushed open her bedroom door. The house was completely quiet, except for the faint rhythmic ticking of the large grandfather clock in the living room downstairs. Ana held her breath as she tiptoed across the hall, but nothing could keep the old boards from creaking and groaning. Ana froze.

Oh, no!

She listened for any sound or movement in the house. Nothing. Finally at her brother's door, Ana leaned her head against the cold, dark oak wood and strained to make out any sound coming from the other side.

You never knew about Connor. Sometimes, he would be up in the middle of the night digging in his closet or playing with the flashlight that Ana had given him for Christmas so he would not need to go looking for hers.

After three minutes, she sighed.

He's got to be asleep.

Skillfully, she pulled on the latch to keep the door from rattling against the jam and at the same time pressed downward until it stopped. Slowly, Ana inched open the door to her brother's room.

Squeak!

Standing motionless in the open doorway, she hoped that the eerie noise had not aroused her brother. By now, her eyes had adjusted to the darkness. There was enough light coming through the window for her to be able to see without using her flashlight.

Connor was sprawled across his bed with one of his pillows in a death clutch. His steady breathing was a combination of deep moans and light snores. Ana shook her head.

Thanks to Andrew, he's probably dreaming about prospecting for gold.

She tiptoed over and knelt down again between his headboard and the wall. Placing the palms of her two hands flat against the panel, she gently but firmly moved it to the left.

Click.

Connor coughed and sat up. Ana froze. Seconds ticked past. Suddenly, he sniffed and lay back down. Finally, deep, rhythmic breathing convinced her he was asleep.

Now.

She pushed the panel open as far as it would go and revealed an almost square, pitch-black opening at least two feet high and not quite two feet wide. Reaching inside the opening,

Ana felt up and down the backside of the panel to determine why it wouldn't open any further.

It's some kind of handle. I need to turn on my flashlight.

Pulling the long, right sleeve of her black kitty cat nightgown out over her hand, she covered the end of the flashlight to dampen the beam and clicked it on. The light filtering through the cloth was bright enough for her to see, but still dark enough that it didn't light up the room. Directing the beam into the darkness, Ana crawled through the opening, which was only as deep as the wall, maybe ten inches. On the other side, it opened up into an area large enough for her to stand up.

Oh, my goodness! It's a secret closet!

Looking around, Ana figured it was about four feet wide and at least eight feet long. At one end, facing her, were two built-in shelves. A large, brown leather suitcase and a smaller, chest-like case were on each shelf.

Behind her, the walls on either side had a similar assortment of men's hang-up clothes: shirts, pants, sweaters, and suits. Underneath the clothes on each wall was a small dresser. After examining the clothes, she determined that they were for two different men. Ana's heart pounded in her chest as the meaning of the discovery dawned on her.

I need to close the panel.

Dropping to her knees, Ana stuck her hand through the opening in the wall, found the handle on the backside of the panel, and slowly, quietly inched it to the left but not all the way shut. Uncovering her flashlight, she stood back up and examined the rest of the small room. On the ceiling above her was a bare lightbulb with a small pull-chain to turn it on.

I wonder if it still works.

She reached up and took hold of the chain, but then stopped.

What am I doing? It's so old that it could pop if I turn it on! Come on, Ana, stay focused!

She shined her light back at the shelves with the suitcases.

Let's see what's in these babies.

Removing the smaller chest from the bottom shelf, she placed it on the floor, held the flashlight in her teeth, undid the brass clasp, and opened it.

What on earth?

Everything was arranged neatly in place. There were three small, plastic bottles, brushes, tubes of make-up, a puffball, bags of hair of different lengths, mustaches, eyebrows, a large, half-spent tube of adhesive, and other items. Even though Ana had never seen anything like this before, she immediately knew what it was.

This was Mr. Griffin's disguise kit!

Embroidered in gold thread into the red satin of the inside of the lid were the initials: *R.M.G.* Ana remembered reading about him using disguises in Beatrice's diaries. Gently, she closed the case, fastened the clasp, and placed it back onto the shelf. Reaching up, she pulled down the other chest from the top shelf and opened it. It was another disguise kit. On the inside of the lid were the initials: *D.D.A.*

"Douglas D. Adams," she whispered. "I wonder what his middle name was."

Closing the kit, she placed it back onto the shelf. Stepping backwards, Ana shined the light around on the floor of the closet and found several pairs of moldy men's leather dress shoes.

Ana was about to open one of the larger suitcases when she heard a noise coming from the other side of the wall. She quickly clicked off her flashlight and stood still in the darkness.

Footsteps. He's up.

Suddenly, light poured through the seam in the panel. Like a cat, Ana crouched down and silently crawled to the passage in the wall. Ana listened for at least a minute but couldn't detect him moving about.

Where is he?

Gripping the backside of the panel, she carefully slid it open. Gradually, Ana eased her head out into the room to look around.

After a few seconds, she almost burst out laughing. Muffled, familiar noises were coming from the hall bathroom. For the first time in her life, Ana was thankful that her little brother was never quiet while going about his business. Hurriedly, she crawled out into the room and slid the panel shut until it clicked. Halfway across the hall, she heard him flush the commode.

Uh, oh!

Springing through the door to her room, Ana waited to close it completely until Connor went stomping past. Minutes later, lying in her bed, she mulled over her recent discovery.

They obviously used Connor's bedroom to change into their disguises, but why store their stuff in a hidden closet?

Ana got out of bed, walked over, and sat down on the built-in, cushioned seat of the large bay window. Wrapping her arms around her knees, she held them close to her chest and lightly leaned the side of her forehead against the windowpane.

Why didn't Griffin just take everything with him after he faked his death and left? Why did he leave it behind?

The rear taillights of a car caught her attention as it slowed down and then pulled into the driveway two houses away further down the street. Ana let go of her knees and moved so she could get a better view. She watched as the garage door slowly opened, and the car disappeared inside.

Oh, my goodness! Maybe he was planning on coming back. But then he couldn't when Dr. Adams was killed in the accident. I wonder if there are other things he left behind.

Ana crawled back into bed. The white numbers of the small digital clock on her nightstand blinked 12:16 am.

"See if you can sniff this out," she whispered softly into the darkness.

There's no way he could have meant the secret closet. If Connor hadn't hit the panel with his bed, I would have never 'sniffed' it out in a million years. And what about the weird drawing? How could it be connected with the closet?

Chapter Twelve

Monday marked the first day of the last week of school before summer break. Everyone was excited and buzzing about the planned events. All Ana wanted to do was get through her classes, meet up with Carter during lunch, and show him the mysterious note. As always, Andrew kept his distance and made sure that she was safe.

After removing the books for her first class, Ana shut the door to her locker and looked straight into the face of Skylar Perkins.

"Oh, uh, good morning," offered Ana kindly. "I really enjoyed seeing you in Sunday School yesterday."

"Really? When you walked into the room and saw me, it was like you were looking at a snake." Skylar was serious. "Which I don't blame you for. I am so sorry about the way I treated you, even after you got my father a job. And I know I've said this before, but this time…" She reached out and held Ana by the arms. "This time I mean it."

Not knowing what else to do, Ana patted her on the arm and stammered. "I'm so glad, Skylar."

"And if you don't want me to come to your slumber party on Friday, I understand. If it were me, I wouldn't want me to come." Ana couldn't explain it, but there was something different about the expression on Skylar's face.

"Oh, no. Please. I want you to come." Ana couldn't believe the words coming out of her mouth, but she was, in some weird way, happy that she had said them.

"Really?" Skylar beamed. "You don't mind?"

"Hey. You are now a member of our Sunday School class, and I invited all the girls which includes you. So, yes. You can come if your parents say it's okay."

"Oh, my parents will say it's okay," she winked. "I haven't changed that much." Both she and Ana burst out laughing. As Ana watched her turn and walk away, she shook her head.

Talk about miracles. I just might start liking Skylar Perkins.

* * * * *

Carter Hudson was already sitting in his usual spot when Ana entered the lunchroom with her tray of food. Andrew, who was right behind her and now such a familiar sight that no one hardly noticed him anymore, sat in his normal place in the corner.

"So did you remember to bring the mysterious card with you?" Carter whispered as she sat down across from him.

"Remember?" she stared at him. "It's just about all I've thought about for the last two days." Which wasn't really true, but Carter didn't need to know everything.

"May I see it?" he grinned. There was something in his tone of voice that caused Ana to wonder if he was taking the whole matter seriously enough. She pulled the envelope out of her pocket and held it out to him underneath the table. "Oh, my," he wiggled in his seat. "This is so exciting."

"If you are just going to make fun, then I'll go sit somewhere else," she groused, but she didn't pull back her hand.

"I'm sorry," he said tenderly. Stretching out his hand underneath the table, he found hers and held it in his. Several seconds passed before he took the note. "After our little adventure in Austria, it's kind of hard to get all worked up about anything anymore."

"Well, I need you to get all worked up about this, please."

"Yes, ma'am. Let me see what I can do," Carter held the envelope below the level of the table so that no one could see it. He carefully removed the small card and examined it. "What do you think this goofy drawing could be?"

"That's what's got me stumped."

"And you are sure that he wrote this the night before he...?" He didn't get to finish his question because Ana interrupted him.

"Yes. I'm sure." She sat straight up, took a drink of water, and looked nervously around the room.

"Oh, don't worry about anyone in here watching us," he snickered. "They'll just think we are passing little love notes back and forth." Immediately, the now familiar reddish tint crept up out of his t-shirt into his cheeks. Ana blushed, too. Carter handed the note to her under the table and grinned. "Here it comes back to you. I put a check mark in the little Yes box where you asked me if I like you, Yes or No."

"You're a mess," she shook her head.

"Don't worry about this mystery," he grinned. "You'll figure it out."

"How can you be so sure?" she asked as she glanced down and slid the note back into her pocket.

"Uh, you're Ana Stilwell."

She looked at him and rolled her eyes. "Well, Ana Stilwell better eat her lunch before it gets cold."

"No kidding," he laughed.

When they were finished, Ana winked at him as she picked up her tray. "Could you go with Andrew and me to the mansion this afternoon?"

"Really? Of course!" he replied as he stood up and grabbed his tray. "Why are we going?"

"There's something that I need the two of you to help me with."

"Ooh, now I'm getting excited again."

Ana jabbed him with her elbow. "I can never tell if you're serious or just joking around."

"Oh, believe me," he leaned forward and spoke softly in her ear. "This time, I'm serious."

* * * * *

When she and Carter exited the front door after school, her little brother was already at the Mercedes standing next to Andrew. Ana paused at the top of the steps to let Carter go ahead of her. When he reached the bottom, she saw him whip out his cell phone to call his parents. She was relieved when he turned around and gave her a thumbs up. Ana trotted down the steps to join him.

"Mom says its fine, but I need to be home in time for dinner."

"It shouldn't us take more than an hour."

She quickly got Andrew's attention and balled her left hand into a fist. Next, she wiped her right hand across her face and held up her right index finger. Ana stuck out the pinky on her left hand and then swiped it up and over her head. Then she balled her left hand into a fist again. With her right hand, she made another wiping movement over her face, followed by a wiggly wave movement out in front of her. Finally, she cupped both hands together.

Andrew tapped the top of his head.

Message received: *First, take her little brother home and then go to the mansion.*

It was a secret sign language that she and Andrew had cooked up, so that they could communicate with each other and hopefully keep her little brother completely in the dark.

"I don't want to go home if you're going to the mansion!" whined Connor. "I want to go, too! Please?"

Ana shot Andrew a disgusted look that he had seen many times before.

What a complete waste of time!

"No," she replied as she walked past him and opened the front passenger door. "You can ride shot-gun on the way home, but you are not going with us to the mansion!"

"Why not?" he grumped as he climbed in the car.

She leaned in and stared at him. "Because you are still recovering from your accident."

"But I feel fine!" Ana shut the door in his face and shook her head at him through the window. Opening the rear door, she got in and grinned at Carter who was already in the car.

Except for some further failed attempts by Connor to get Ana to change her mind, the ride to the Stilwells' house was uneventful, if not quiet. As they pulled into the driveway, however, her brother's appeals increased in volume.

"It's not fair! It's just not fair!"

Ana's mother was waiting in the driveway. Connor was still hollering as the car rolled to a stop. Nancy Stilwell opened the door and grabbed him by the arm.

"Stop fussing!" she scolded and pulled him out. "It's your own fault for trying to jump from the chair to your bed." She held him tightly with one arm and waved at the trio in the Mercedes with the other as Andrew backed the car out of the driveway.

"Why can't he go with us?" asked Carter as they pulled out into the street.

"You don't know him like we do," joked Andrew. He checked the rearview mirror.

"Mom wanted him to come straight home after school," explained Ana. "And, anyway, I don't want him to see what I'm going to show you. Oh yeah," she reached up and lightly touched Andrew's shoulder, "We need to first run by Shane's Hardware store and get a long tarp."

"A tarp? For what? Why do we need a tarp?"

Ana glanced up at Andrew's wide-eyed reflection in the rearview mirror and grinned.

"You'll see."

* * * * *

At the mansion, Andrew retrieved the long, blue 7' X 20' plastic tarp from the trunk. "So, what do we do now?" he inquired as he closed the lid.

"We go this way." Ana took the lead with Carter close at her heels. Andrew, still mumbling, brought up the rear.

"I can't figure out why we need this thing," he said as he shifted it from under his left arm to underneath his right arm. "People usually use them as a drop cloth when they're painting or something."

"My dad's got one that we put dish detergent on and then wet it down with the hose to make a slip-and-slide in the backyard," laughed Carter. When they reached the overgrown edge of the orchard, Ana stopped and looked at him.

"A slip-and-slide," she smiled and pointed at Andrew. "But one without water! Why, that's exactly what this is."

"What are you talking about?" he wiped the sweat from his forehead.

"You'll see," she snickered and kept walking. "Watch your step."

Chapter Thirteen

Unlike on Saturday, this time Ana walked straight to the trap door hidden in the orchard.

"Look!" remarked Andrew, pointing at the matted down grass and weeds. "Some animal has been bedding down here."

"You think?" She got down on her knees, pushed the weeds to the side, inserted her fingers into the latch and pulled backwards.

Clunk.

The large rectangular metal door popped open before their eyes.

"Oh, wow. This is wild!" exclaimed Carter.

"Uh, no. This is normal," muttered Andrew as he knelt down next to Ana, who was busy clearing away weeds. "Here. Let me do that."

"Gladly," she said and stood back up.

Her huge bodyguard had no trouble pushing open the large metal plate as far as it would go. Carter moved over and stood next to Ana. The three of them peered down into the hole.

Nudging her in the side, Carter said, "It's some kind of ramp!" Ana smiled but didn't say anything. This was the real reason she wanted him to come along, so that she could enjoy watching his reaction to each thrilling development.

"Where's the tarp?" Ana looked at Andrew.

"Right here," he picked it up and showed it to her. "I have a bad feeling about this."

"Would you two please unroll it?"

When they were finished, Carter wiped his hands, "Now what?"

"You just had to ask, didn't you?" groaned Andrew.

Ana motioned with her hands back and forth. "Spread it out, over, and down the ramp as far as it will go."

"Down the ramp?" laughed Carter. "Are you serious?"

"Yes," grumbled Andrew. "She's serious."

"This way," explained Ana, gesturing with her hands, "we won't get filthy dirty when we…"

"When we slip and slide down into who knows what!" Carter finished the sentence for her.

Andrew stared at him. "Oh, no," he motioned with his thumb toward Ana. "She knows exactly what's down there."

Carter turned to her. His eyes were as wide open as a twelve-year-old boy's eyes could get.

"Seriously? You've already been down there? By yourself? Weren't you scared to death?"

"Her? Scared?" Andrew howled. "That'll be the day."

Ana rolled her eyes at him. "Can we please get on with it?" She pulled her flashlight out of her pocket and clicked it on. "There's something down there that I need to show you."

"Yes, ma'am!" Andrew and Carter replied in unison. "We're on it." Ana watched as they stood on either side of the tarp and carefully guided it down the ramp. She followed the progress with her flashlight.

"Stop. That's perfect," she said. "It goes all the way to the end."

"We'll need something heavy to hold it in place up here—to keep it from sliding down," noted Andrew, surveying the area. "Like a large rock or a heavy limb."

"How about putting some sticks through these grommets and jamming them into the ground?" suggested Carter pointing at the metal reinforced holes in the tarp.

Andrew agreed. "That should work." Ana watched as they broke thin but sturdy limbs off a nearby shrub and skinned the leaves off. Andrew pulled out his pocket-knife and sharpened the ends.

"Here you go," he handed it to Carter and motioned toward the tarp. "Put it through the grommet hole on that corner and shove it in the ground."

"Check." When he was finished, he looked up at Andrew, who was just finishing another peg. "I'll hold it while you pull the tarp tight and secure your side."

"10-4." Andrew pulled and inserted the homemade stake through the grommet and pushed it into the ground. Standing up, he joined Carter and Ana to admire their finished work.

"Not bad," she smiled. "So, who's going down first?" Both men cleared their throats but didn't budge. "What a couple of ninnies!" Ana squatted down, held her flashlight out in front of her, and pushed off. Worried that she would zip to the bottom, Ana was a little disappointed when, instead, she had to use her outstretched legs and feet to keep moving downward.

"Come on Carter!" she called from the bottom. "If you wait on Andrew, we'll be here all day!"

"Very funny!" Her huge bodyguard slowly inched his way down the ramp.

"Wee! Wee! Wee! All the way home!" Ana cried and then burst out laughing. When he reached the bottom Andrew shook his head.

"Have I ever told you that you are a riot?"

"Several times."

"Look out below!" shouted Carter. Ana watched as he made it all the way down without stopping.

"Watch your step. It's kinda messy down here." She shined her light around on the ground so they wouldn't step into a pile of something.

"Oh, my," Andrew sniffed. "What an interesting smell."

It didn't take long for their eyes to adjust to the darkness. With the light pouring down the ramp and the beams seeping in through the steel grates in the ceiling, Ana knew they wouldn't need her flashlight for the time being, so she clicked it off. She didn't say a word and enjoyed watching Andrew and Carter as they scanned the gigantic underground chamber.

"What is this place?" asked Carter in a hushed tone. Andrew touched him on the shoulder.

"This is where she found Ricky."

Ana pointed out the water trough, running along one of the walls.

"How long was he in here?" asked Carter.

"At least twenty years—probably more," she said and gestured toward one of the steel grates in the ceiling. "Mr. Griffin built these so that fruit from the trees would drop through. Ricky lived off apples, pears, leaves and twigs. The trough captured a small, underground stream so he had plenty of water."

"This is unreal." Carter shook his head. "Look," he said, motioning with his hand. "Most of the walls are reinforced with concrete blocks."

Andrew leaned over to Ana and asked, "So, why did you bring us down here?"

"I'll show you." She led them out of the light toward a much darker part of the room. Clicking on her flashlight again, Ana revealed the opening to the tunnel.

"Oh, wow!" exclaimed Carter.

"Get used to saying 'Wow'," muttered Andrew.

They entered the tunnel and kept walking as it sloped gradually downward. Finally, they reached the strange-looking metal gate that blocked their way.

"Mr. Griffin obviously put this in to stop Ricky. I call it 'Ricky's Gate'." Ana shined the light on the long, odd-looking latch contraption that ran along the left wall on the other side. "There is no way he could have accidently opened it."

"How do we get through?" asked Carter.

"We don't," said Andrew. "Unless you have an arm that's eight feet long or a long pole with a hook on it." He motioned to Ana. "May I borrow your flashlight?"

"Sure." She handed it to him and watched as he peered through the gate and examined the locking latch. "Looks easy enough to open." He shined the light to see her face.

"You were on the other side when you found this, weren't you?" Ana nodded. Carter almost said something but didn't.

She looked at Andrew and motioned with her head toward Carter. "He was with us in Austria. I think he needs to know everything."

"You're the boss."

She put her hand on Carter's shoulder. "You'll need to keep all of this a secret, too."

Chapter Fourteen

Directing the light past Ricky's Gate into the darkness, Ana began. "This tunnel leads to a large room which is the hub of the whole tunnel system," she began. "From there, a long tunnel goes to a hidden workroom next to the cellar. Another tunnel goes from the cellar to underneath the mausoleum." Ana pushed her hair behind her ear with her hand and moved the flashlight to the right. "Back at the large room again, there is very long tunnel that goes all the way to a hidden entrance at the creek."

"The creek behind your house?"

"Exactly."

Carter couldn't take his eyes off her as she talked, and Ana was enjoying every second. "Another tunnel goes from the large room to a door and a stairway. At the top is a narrow passageway which leads to a secret entrance into the mansion. It's in a panel in the wall in a hall in the rear of the mansion.". The two of them stood there for moment. Nobody said or moved. Finally, Carter inched closer to her. Ana shined the light so she could see him. His eyes were gleaming.

"Wow!" he whispered.

nted at Carter. "He hasn't seen ansion since you've had it all up, has he?" Ana shook her head.

saw that huge entrance hall and main dining room at your twelfth birthday party. Remember?" Andrew bent over, stared him in the face, and grinned.

"Little brother, you ain't seen nothing, yet!" He turned around, looked at Ana, and motioned with his head. "So, why did you want us to see this gate?" She turned and headed back toward Ricky's Palace.

"Last Saturday, after Connor's party, I came over here, found the trap door and realized that Ricky has been bedding down on top of it. While I was there, he crawled up and began nudging the door with his nose and making noises. I'm sure he wants to get back down in here." When they entered the large chamber, she clicked off her flashlight and kept walking until they reached the bottom of the ramp. "I just want him to be happy," she explained and pointed up at the opening. "But if I leave the trap door open, then anyone could find it."

"And have access to the rest of the tunnels," added Andrew, rubbing his chin.

"Exactly."

Andrew continued, "Ricky's gate won't stop anyone determined to get through it."

"I agree," she said. He let out a deep breath and stared at her.

"We could seal off the tunnel with a concrete wall, but that would mean changing it, and I already know how you feel about that."

Ana shook her head. "No. I don't want to do that, unless there is absolutely no other way." After several seconds, she gazed up at him. "How hard would it be to seal it off like you said?"

Andrew stepped away from them and surveyed the room.

"It would be quite a big project." He wiped his forehead on his sleeve. "We would need to use the same size concrete blocks and then somehow make it blend in to hide it." He turned around and stared at her. "And we'll have to do it all by ourselves, since you don't want more people to know what's down here.

"I could help," Carter piped up. "My dad and I built a retaining wall out of concrete blocks behind our garage last summer, so I know how to mix mortar and lay blocks."

"You might ought to ask Chuck what he thinks before you decide," suggested Andrew.

"That's a good idea." She walked past him to the bottom of the ramp and pointed. "So, how do we get out of here?"

Andrew joined her and scratched his head. "Uh…" He picked up the end of the tarp. "Why don't you and Carter roll this up in front of you as you climb out. Don't pull on it, just use it to keep your balance."

"That ought to work," said Carter. "Let's try it!" He and Ana stood next to each other, held on to the tarp, and began carefully rolling it up as they slowly scaled the ramp.

"This is great!" she declared. "Good thinking, Mr. Collins!"

"Is that his last name?" asked Carter and glanced over at her. Ana nodded. "That is wild!" he exclaimed. "We spent all that time in Austria together, and I never knew his last name!" Ana laughed and kept climbing.

When they got to the top, she called back down to her bodyguard. "So, how are you going to get out?"

Motioning with his hands, Andrew said, "Hang on to your end, unroll the tarp, and send it back down to me." Ana and Carter did as he requested. Andrew picked up his end of it. "Okay. Now, both of you stand on it while I try to get out. If you see it slipping, holler!"

"Okay! We're ready!" she shouted. "Just please don't yank us back down the ramp!"

"Very funny," came Andrew's muffled reply from below. "Here I come. I'll use the tarp to keep my balance as I climb out. Don't let it slip."

"We won't!" they called. Seconds later, Andrew emerged through the opening and grabbed the side of the metal frame and used it to pull himself out.

"Ugh!" he groaned as he stood up. "What a pain!" Ana could tell he wasn't finished and let him catch his breath. "We're going to need to get a long ladder or something to be able to get in and out of this hole. I am done with this slip-and-slide stuff." While she and Carter folded up the tarp, he lowered the large trap door back into position and stepped on it to make sure it was shut.

"If I do decide to wall off the tunnel, how long do you think it will take?" she asked as they made their way back to the Mercedes.

"That depends," Andrew explained from behind.

"What do you mean?" she asked without turning around.

"Well, we can get Shane's Hardware to deliver the concrete blocks and the bags of mortar, but we'll need them to unload everything at the edge of the parking lot."

"Why is that?" Ana asked as she and Carter stopped to look at him.

"Because that way they won't know what it's for."

"Oh, yeah. Right." When they reached the parking lot, she stopped. "But if they unload the stuff here, how do we get it over to where the trap door is?"

"With a wheelbarrow." Andrew held his two hands out in front of him like he was holding on to imaginary handles.

Carter spoke up. "We'll also need a concrete mixer or a large tub to mix the mortar in." He used his fingers to rattle off more necessary items. "And a shovel, a hoe, a couple of five-gallon buckets, a trowel, a mortar board, and a level."

"And a long water hose with water in it," added Andrew. Ana let out a deep sigh, as he opened the trunk of the car, tossed in the tarp, and closed the lid.

"I'll call Chuck when I get home." She opened the back door of the car. "Maybe he can think of something else."

"I surely hope so," said Andrew. As the Mercedes' motor roared to life, Carter moved over next to her on the back seat until his shoulder was lightly touching hers. Ana looked up at the rearview mirror: Andrew was watching them. His eyes were going back and forth. She quickly gave him her "stop it" stare.

"Thanks for asking me to come," Carter said softly, "and for telling me everything."

"I hope you don't mind me getting you so involved in all of this." Ana rubbed her nose. He grinned at her.

"Are you kidding? I wouldn't miss it for the world!"

Chapter Fifteen

"If we do have to seal up the tunnel in Ricky's Palace, how are you going to explain it to your parents?" Ana asked as they pulled up in front of Carter's house.

"Uh," he furrowed his brow. "I've got it. I'll tell them, uh, that I'm helping you build a wall on your estate—which is true. Right?"

Ana chuckled, "Isn't that what you call *creative truth telling*?"

"Me? What about you?" Carter rolled his eyes and tried to sound like her. "Oh, during spring break I'll be checking out an old building near a river, instead of, Oh, I'll be jetting over to Vienna, Austria to check out a medieval castle on the Danube River to see if some really old rich dude is still alive."

Ana and Andrew both jerked in their seats and glared at him. Ana shook her head violently back and forth.

"Stop! You can't ever mention him again!"

"Not even to you guys?"

"No! Not to us or anyone, ever!" Ana wagged her head. "Boy! You need to learn how to keep a secret a secret!"

"Listen to her, son," advised Andrew. "She's a professional!"

"Sorry," he held up his right hand. "I promise to never, ever mention again, uh, what I just mentioned. Scout's honor!"

"Are you a Boy Scout?" Andrew glared.

"No." His cheeks were blood red. "That's just what my dad always says whenever he promises my mom something." He got out of the car, turned around, poked his head back in, bit his lower lip, and winced at Ana. "Will you forgive me?"

"Forgive you for what?" she grinned. "I'll let you know if and when we begin the project. Thanks for all your help today."

"My pleasure!" He gently closed the car door and trotted across his yard. At the front porch, he turned and waved. She waved at him as Andrew pulled out into the traffic.

"He's a good kid. You know that?"

Ana was still smiling and waving at him.

"He's wonderful."

* * * * *

Back at the house, Ana went straight to her room. Standing in front of the mirror, she noticed a revolting smell wafting around her.

"Whew!" she held her nose. "What is that smell?" Bending over, she checked out the legs of her jeans. They were splattered with filth. "Ricky's Palace!" she groaned. "I need a bath!" After getting undressed, Ana put on her bathrobe, grabbed her dirty clothes, and headed for the bathroom. After tossing everything into the hamper, she walked over, got a can of strong citrus-smelling room deodorant off the shelf, sprayed several shots into the hamper, and snickered.

I wonder how long it'll take Andrew and Carter to realize that they are the ones stinking up the place.

* * * * *

Clean, dressed, and back in her bedroom, Ana pulled out her cell phone and tapped in Chuck's number.

"I'm so glad you called," he said when he answered. "I was about to call you."

"Really, what's up?" she asked.

"You first," he countered.

"It's quite a list."

"That's okay. Remember, I work for you. So, what have you got?"

Ana sighed. "Okay. First, Andrew, Carter and I went over to the mansion today, to the orchard. We opened up the trap door to Ricky's Palace, and..."

"Trap door to Ricky's Palace?" he interrupted her. "What are you talking about?"

"It's a huge room underneath the orchard where I found Ricky," she paused to let him catch his breath. "Uh, do you remember the large room I showed you and Andrew? The one where I found the skeleton key?"

"Yes," he stated matter-of-factly. "Go on."

"Do you remember seeing another tunnel? I'm not talking about the one that goes to the creek. It was to the left of the tunnel with the door and the staircase."

"I remember seeing the other tunnel. Yes."

"Well, it leads to Ricky's Palace. That's what Lewis Griffin called it."

"And?"

"Last Saturday, at Connor's birthday party, after you, Mom, and Dad left, I went over to the orchard. There is a trap door. It's how I let Ricky out of his palace."

"And?" he said calmly. Ana could tell he was making notes.

"Well, I think he wants to get back into his home, where he lived for so many years. But I can't just leave the trap door open because someone could find it and find the other tunnels. So, that's why Andrew, Carter, and I slid down a tarp that we put on the ramp that's underneath the trap door. But after talking about it, Andrew said that the only way to keep people from finding the other tunnels would be to build a concrete wall and seal the room off. But that is going to take a ton of work, and we'll have to do it all by ourselves so that nobody knows."

Chuck let out a deep sigh. "Right," he said calmly. "Can you meet me at the mansion tomorrow after school and show me what you are talking about?"

"That would be great!" she cried. "You'll need to wear old clothes because it's pretty dirty down there."

"I'll be fine," he stated. "And I will bring some rope, so that we can lower ourselves down the ramp instead of sliding down." Ana imagined Chuck flying down the tarp and almost burst out laughing.

"Now, why didn't I think of that?" she giggled. "That makes a lot more sense. You should have seen Andrew today. It was hilarious!" Ana hesitated. "Uh, do you mind if Carter comes, too?" she asked sheepishly.

Careful to use his lawyer's voice, Chuck replied. "He is your friend, so, if you want him to come, he is more than welcome." After a brief pause, he asked, "Okay. So, what else is on your list?"

Ana mentioned needing him to help her get things ready for her slumber party at the mansion on Friday and Saturday.

"I've already spoken with your mother about that," explained Chuck. "I'm sure it won't be a problem. What else?"

"I want to buy the two houses next to ours so that I own all the land that borders the creek behind our house."

"May I ask why?"

"I don't want anyone prowling around down there because they might find the secret door in the boulder and the tunnel to the mansion," she explained.

"The one you didn't have time to show us when we were with you in the tunnels?" asked Chuck.

"Exactly," said Ana.

"Let me see what I can do," noted Chuck. "Uh, anything else?"

Ana sighed, "I want to use half of my money to help poor people have good paying jobs so that they won't be poor anymore. If we can't find them jobs, then I want to do whatever it takes to get them a job."

Chuck swallowed hard. "You do realize that you're talking about a very large sum of money, right?"

"Yes. But it's something I really want to do," she said firmly.

"May I ask where you got the idea to do this?"

"From Zacchaeus in the Bible. He told Jesus that he was going to give half of what he owned to the poor. We studied about it in Sunday School. I figured if he did it, then I could, too."

"Yes, ma'am," Chuck coughed. "I'll see what I can come up with and give you a report on Friday at our meeting."

"Could we move our meeting up to Thursday this week?" she asked. "I figure we'll be too busy on Friday with my slumber party."

"That is why I was going to call you, to suggest that very thing."

Ana laughed, "Great minds think alike."

Chuck let out a deep breath. "Was there anything—else—on your list?"

"Oh, yes," she remembered. "I need you to please find an animal doctor, who can examine Ricky." The tone of her voice turned serious.

"That's not a bad idea," agreed Chuck. Several seconds passed. Ana could tell he was writing. "Okay. Uh, I doubt that anyone in the state or even in the southeast would be qualified," he explained. "We may need to fly in an expert from the Galapagos Islands."

"Whatever it takes. I promised Rudolph Griffin that I would take care of him, and I mean to do it, regardless of how much it costs."

"Yes, ma'am. I understand. I'll get right on it."

"Thank you so much," she said sweetly. "I don't know what I would do without you. I'll let Andrew and Carter know that we're meeting you tomorrow at the mansion. I'm sure Andrew will be glad you are bringing a rope."

"Why don't we just surprise him?"

Ana laughed, "I can't wait to see his face. See you tomorrow."

* * * * *

After ending the call, Ana walked over and sat down on the seat of the bay window. For at least a half an hour she stared aimlessly down at the street watching people and the traffic.

A silver BMW crept slowly past their house. Ana noticed that the driver was staring out the window in her direction.

Oh, my goodness! That looks like Lawrence Hill!

Chapter Sixteen

Kneeling quickly on the window seat, Ana pressed her head against the pane to get a better look. It was a man driving, but the glare of the setting sun glinting off the side window made it impossible to confirm her suspicion.

What am I doing?

Immediately, Ana jumped back and moved to the left side of the window.

I wonder if he saw me.

Slowly, she inched closer so that she could see down the street. The car was gone. Ana stood there frozen, wondering if he might come back. A minute later, she got her answer as the same car passed by again—this time from left to right. The driver was on the other side of the vehicle, so it was impossible to be sure it was Hill, but it was a silver BMW.

Why is he driving back and forth in front of our house? Is he stalking me or something? What does he want?

"Ana! Connor!" called her father from downstairs. "Supper's ready! Come on!"

"Coming!"

As she descended the steps, Ana recognized a familiar aroma coming from the kitchen and quickened her pace.

Mom's grilled cheese sandwiches.

Not wanting to upset anyone, and since she had not been able positively to identify Lewistowne's most famous lawyer, she decided to keep to herself what had just occurred.

"So, what did you do today, Ana?" her father asked after he ended the prayer for their meal.

"She and Andrew and Carter Hudson went over to the mansion!" blurted out Connor. "But I didn't get to go!"

"Quiet, dear," said Ana's mother.

"The mansion?" Ronnie Stilwell followed the pointed inquiry with a spoonful of tomato soup. Ana didn't respond, but instead waited for him to swallow. "What were you doing? Making plans for your slumber party?" He glanced over at Ana's mother.

"I hope you don't mind," Nancy took over. "I went ahead and phoned Chuck to help with preparations. He talked with your Sunday School teacher, and she said that every girl in your class will be coming. Nine girls in all. Ten counting you."

"Mrs. Thompson's coming, too," added Ana, thankful that her father had answered his own question about why she, Andrew, and Carter had been at the mansion.

"Oh, that's nice of you." Something in her mother's tone of voice let Ana know that she also wanted to be invited.

"Mom, would you mind coming, too? That way we would have enough adults in the mansion to…"

"To keep you girls from wrecking the place!" snipped Connor. "That's why you won't let me and my friends spend the night in there like I wanted to. It's not fair! It's just not fair!"

Ana glared at him. "Listen, Mr. Smarty Pants. You have no idea what my life is like. I have to deal with people constantly staring at me and living under guard every second I'm awake. I have more responsibilities and more pressure on me than a little worm like you could ever imagine!" She paused only to reload. "So, if I want to have a slumber party with my Sunday School class in my mansion, then that is what I am going to do, and you had better not try to ruin it for me. Have I made myself clear?" Tears were flowing down her face. "Just see if I ever throw you a huge birthday party again." Ana glanced over at her parents. Their mouths were gaping open. Bursting into tears, she stood up and raced out of the room just as Andrew was entering. He stood to the side to avoid her running into him.

"What did I miss?" he held up his hands.

Ana ran upstairs to her room and closed the door. Minutes later, her mother knocked on it.

"May I come in?" Ana was embarrassed that she had made such a scene. Wiping her tears away from her eyes, she opened the door and fell into her mother's arms.

After a long pause, Nancy Stilwell asked tenderly. "What's wrong?"

"I apologize," she sniffed. "I shouldn't have unloaded on him like that, but sometimes he can be so..."

"Childish?" Her mother laughed. "Yes. He can be very exasperating at times, but I get the feeling that there is more going on here than just being upset with your brother. What's really the matter?"

"Oh, it's a lot of things." Ana sniffed again.

"Here." Her mother produced a small package of tissues from her pocket and pulled one out. "Wipe your nose."

They sat down on the edge of the bed.

"There's just so much going on right now, and I don't know what I want to do," Ana said.

"Is this about your slumber party?"

"Oh, no." Ana shook her head. "I'm ready to just hire a maid and have all the food catered. That way you can direct everything without having to do the work."

Her mother grinned. "I would love to, but if it's not the slumber party, then what's really bothering you?"

Ana sat up and stared at her mother. "Do you remember when we re-buried Rudolph Griffin?"

"That I will never forget," she rolled her eyes.

"Well, underneath the mausoleum is a tunnel." Ana saw her mother's eyes widen. "That's how Mr. Griffin got out. Mom, there are tunnels running everywhere underneath the estate. One goes from the creek to the mansion, which is how I got inside." Nancy Stilwell put her hand over her mouth. Ana figured it was time to come clean, well, cleaner. "There's another one that goes to a big room underneath the orchard where I found Ricky—the tortoise," she paused. Her mother took her hand away from her mouth.

"I know who Ricky is," she chuckled.

"Well, in the orchard there is a trap door with a ramp that leads down into the room. I want Ricky to be able to go in and out of it whenever he wants to, but I don't want to leave the trap door open, because then anybody could find it. That's why I didn't want the lawn service to clean up that side of the mansion."

"Oh," muttered her mother. "Now it makes sense. Your father and I wondered about that."

Ana held out her hands. "Andrew says we could build a concrete wall to block off the tunnel, but that would be a ton of work, which we would have to do all by ourselves."

"Because you don't want anyone to know about it," sighed her mother.

"Right," Ana put her head into her hands. "Ricky is so old, and I promised Mr. Griffin that I would look after him. I asked Chuck to find him a doctor, but I'll probably have to fly one in from the Galapagos Islands."

"What does Chuck say about building the wall Andrew was talking about?"

"We're supposed to meet at the mansion tomorrow and make a decision. Oh, my goodness!" Ana sprang to her feet. "I need to text Carter to see if he can come."

"Carter Hudson?" Nancy's voice had an interesting tone to it. "So, he was with you?"

"Yes, ma'am." Ana shot her a sheepish grin as she tapped in his number. "He's the only fun part about this whole mess." When Ana finished, Nancy stood up and walked to the door. "Come on. Let's go back downstairs."

When they walked into the kitchen, Connor jumped up, ran to Ana, and hugged her. "I'm sorry I made you so mad. I want you to have a nice party." He stared up at her. She had seen this look many times before. "Please don't banish me from your estate." Everyone held their breath for as long as they could but then howled with laughter.

"How about some ice cream?" Nancy held up a carton of chocolate mint. Connor let go of Ana and whirled around.

"I want two scoops!" he cried.

Ana walked over and hugged her father. "What's that for?" he asked.

"I'll tell you later," she whispered.

* * * * *

Later that night, Ana lay in bed staring out her bay window, talking with God.

"Dear Lord, please help me to not blow up at Connor like I did tonight. Thank you for Chuck. Let me know what to do about Ricky's Palace and help us find a tortoise doctor for him. Please let us know how to help poor people find good jobs Thank you for Mom and Dad and Andrew and Carter. Thank you that something good has happened to Skylar. Please lead me and guide me with your Spirit and show me what you want me to do. In Jesus name I pray. Amen."

She turned over and closed her eyes.

And please protect me from Lawrence Hill.

Chapter Seventeen

Tuesday morning, Ana walked into the kitchen and couldn't believe her eyes. Connor's normally brown hair had been dyed a hideous green and purple and shaped into long, dangerous-looking spikes. He turned around and stared at her like there was something wrong with her.

"You can't go to school like that! It's Wild Hair Tuesday!" he shouted.

Ana plopped down in her seat at the breakfast table. She had completely forgotten. Pajamas Day was on Wednesday and Throwback Thursday was, well, on Thursday. She was fine with them, but Ana secretly detested Wild Hair Day. They had done the same thing in her old school back in Braxton, and she despised it then. Her mother walked over and touched her on the shoulder.

"Go put your hair up in three pony-tails with different colored hair ties," she suggested.

"But that's not wild enough," her little brother protested over a mouth full of cereal. "You won't win a prize!" Ana pointed at his head.

"One of your spikes is drooping."

Immediately, Connor began gently touching his hair, twisting back and forth, struggling to see them. "Which one?" he demanded. Her mother came to his rescue with more gel.

"Stop jerking around and let me fix it."

As Ana ate her cereal, her thoughts drifted to Carter Hudson and his perfect hair and then, sadly enough, back to her immediate future. She shook her head and took another bite.

Why does it have to be Wild Hair Day?

* * * * *

When she came back downstairs, her hair was done up in three ponytails. Andrew was waiting on her, sporting a fuzzy, black wig.

"Who do you think you are?" she howled. "Bob Ross?"

"Who?"

"You know—happy, little trees?"

"Oh, yeah. Right," he laughed.

She snickered, "I can't believe that you're taking part in Wild Hair Day."

"I heard the kids talking about it yesterday. I thought it might help me to blend in."

"When did you have time to get that wig?"

"I got it a couple of years ago when I was practicing disguises for my police work."

Ana halted in her tracks and thought about the hidden closet in Connor's bedroom. She leaned in closer to her bodyguard so that her little brother couldn't hear.

"Remind me later to show you something else I found."

* * * * *

Wild Hair Day back in Braxton was tame compared to what Ana now saw as she made her way down the halls. Students, teachers, office workers, and even Mr. Cobb, the custodian, were showing off their exotic hairdos. The usually reserved school principal, Mrs. Moore, had her hair done up like a gigantic, frosted donut with colored sprinkles. Just before entering her first class, Ana spied Carter Hudson coming toward her through the crowded hall. His hair was completely normal.

"What happened?" she said as he got closer.

"I forgot it was Wild Hair Day. Can you believe it? I guess I was so churned up from spending the afternoon with you and Andrew that it didn't cross my mind." Ana smiled, reached up and yanked the colored hair ties out, releasing her ponytails. Carter watched as she took her fingers and fluffed her hair.

"How's that?" she grinned.

"Perfect," he approved.

"Now you're not the only one who forgot." She turned around and got Andrew's attention. Ana motioned at his head. He immediately removed the black fuzzy wig and crammed it into his pocket.

Spinning back around she winked at Carter. "Now, there are three of us."

* * * * *

Ana's mother had taken Connor to school that morning in their SUV and was now waiting on him to take him home. Ana had overheard her explaining to him that she didn't want him getting hair gel on the inside of the Mercedes. Ana was glad that they could avoid the scene from the previous day. She waved when she saw Carter appear through the front door.

"Mom said I could go with you to the mansion whenever you ask me," he called. "I just need to let them know."

"Well, that's good news."

As they rode along, Ana poked Carter with her elbow. "It's a good thing you forgot about Wild Hair Day, huh?"

"Why is that?"

"Well, imagine if, say, you had spikes all over your head like Connor, and we got stopped by the police because Andrew rolled through a stop sign," she teased.

"Uh, excuse me!" her bodyguard corrected. "I do not roll through stop signs. I come to a full stop every time."

"It was only a hypothetical situation."

"Well, I would appreciate you coming up with something else, if you don't mind."

"Please forgive me. I apologize. You are an excellent driver." She grinned at Carter. "Okay, how's this? We all have wild hair, and suddenly, there is a guy breaking into a car. You jump out, arrest him, and your old police buddies come get him. Imagine what they would say if we were all goofed up, and you were wearing your black fuzzy Bob Ross wig?"

"I'm never going to live that down, am I?"

Ana winked at Carter, "Probably not."

Minutes later, they cruised through the service gate at the former Griffin estate. Chuck was waiting for them on the other side.

"I'll close the gate," he waved. "We don't want to chance Ricky getting out."

* * * * *

Later in the parking lot, when Chuck produced a 50-foot length of brand-new rope that was as thick as a garden hose, Ana could tell that Andrew was relieved. "That's more like it!" he exclaimed.

When they arrived at the trap door, Andrew unlatched and pushed it open.

"Carter, help me tie this end of the rope to that apple tree," said Chuck. When they finished, Andrew tossed the rest of the rope down the ramp.

Waving his arms, Andrew said, "Okay, everybody stand back and let me show you how it's done." Holding on to the rope, he began repelling backwards down the ramp. He stared straight at Ana. "I'm going first, so I will be able to catch you if you get scared and let go."

"I don't know what I would do without you," she called. Ana went next and made it down in half the time it took Andrew. Carter was next followed by Chuck. Ana clicked on her flashlight.

"This is unreal," muttered Chuck.

"Let me show you the little challenge we have down here," she said and led the group toward the other end of the huge underground chamber.

* * * * *

After checking out the tunnel and the metal gate, they returned to the bottom of the ramp.

"I've racked my brain to come up with a different solution other than walling off the tunnel, but I keep drawing a blank," Andrew said holding out his hands.

Chuck stared at Ana. "Why are you afraid to just leave the trap door open? Why does it matter if everyone knows about the tunnels?"

"Are you serious?" she exclaimed.

"Completely," nodded Chuck. "I could understand you wanting to keep everything a secret when you found out Rudolph Griffin wasn't dead, because of the nature of his first will. And I can understand you now wanting to protect his reputation by not letting anyone know what he did."

"I'm listening." Ana clicked off her flashlight.

"Even if someone does find the tunnels," Chuck explained, "there is still that massive metal plate that blocks the way to the cellar and on to the mausoleum. No one can get past that. The door up to the secret entrance into the mansion is locked, and you are the only one with the key!"

Ana turned toward Carter. "I'll show you later what he's talking about, if you want me to."

He laughed, "Oh, I want to see everything!"

Ana directed her attention back to Chuck. "So, please continue. Why doesn't it matter that everyone knows about the tunnels?"

Chuck leaned over and smiled at her. "Because you, my dear Miss Stilwell, have another will personally signed by Rudolph Griffin himself, which names you as his sole heir! It is certified with a notary public seal from Austria to remove any shadow of doubt. You, young lady, have absolutely no reason to fear anything or anyone, ever. Why you could even give tours of the place if you wanted to."

Suddenly, above their heads a deep, scraping sound made them turn around. An enormous, rounded-shaped something, silhouetted against the bright sky cast an eerie shadow as it slowly inched its way down the ramp.

"Well, look who's here!" cried Ana. Everyone backed away as Ricky scraped and slid toward them. Ana figured he would stop at the bottom, but instead, he kept crawling.

"Where's he going?" asked Carter.

"Let's wait and find out," replied Andrew.

"I agree," said Ana as she clicked her flashlight back on. The ancient reptile slowly made a wide but very determined left turn toward one of the darkest corners of the room. "Oh, look!" She shined the light in front of him. A large, but wallowed out mucky mound of leaves, twigs, and who knows what else, was clearly recognizable. "That must be his nest! No wonder he wanted to come back down here!" Just before reaching the mound, however, Ricky veered off to the right.

"Hey!" called Andrew. "Where are you going?" Ignoring the question, Ricky didn't stop until he reached the wall. Suddenly, he began making a series of deep, soft grunting noises. After that, a faint, rhythmic thumping sound began echoing through the chamber.

Tap. Tap. Tap.

"He's hitting his nose against the wall," stated Chuck. Ana inched closer and aimed her light at the spot where he was tapping. The marks left by the tortoise's nose on the dirty surface caused her to shriek out loud.

"Oh, wow! Look!" she cried, pointing excitedly at the smudges. "It's the weird drawing on the card! It's Ricky's nose!" Handing the flashlight to Chuck, Ana bent over and lovingly put her hands on both sides of the tortoise's head.

"This is unbelievable!" exclaimed Chuck. He moved closer and shined the light at the wall above Ricky's head.

Tap. Tap. Tap.

"Look! Some of these joints are cracked!" He followed the broken seams with his finger. Chuck turned and looked at Ana's bodyguard. "What do you make of this?"

Andrew stepped forward. "It's not unusual for concrete block walls to have cracked seams," he gestured with his hand, "but these don't appear to be random."

"What do you mean?" asked Ana as she stood back up.

Tap. Tap. Tap.

"I wonder," said Andrew and took a step backwards. "Chuck, would you please shine the light on the floor at the base of the wall?"

"No problem."

The floor was filthy just like everywhere else. Andrew used his foot to scrape away some of the debris.

"Why are you doing that?" asked Carter.

"Just a hunch. I wanted to see if this might be some kind of door. But there's no indication here that it was ever opened in this direction." Ana and the three men silently studied the scene in front of them.

Tap. Tap. Tap.

"So, then why does he keep tapping on it?" asked Carter.

Ana motioned to Chuck. "May I have my flashlight for a second?"

"Here you go."

Shining the light back onto the wall, Ana moved closer.

"Do you know what I think?"

She lightly rubbed her hand across the rough concrete surface.

"Here we go," mumbled Andrew, nudging Carter in the side. Ana turned and shined the light so that the others could see her face.

"I think Ricky is hoping that Mr. Griffin, or Dr. Adams, or maybe even Lewis will come through the wall right here—just like they used to. This has got to be what Mr. Griffin wanted me to find. There must be something on the other side of this wall. Now all I have to do is *sniff* out what it is."

"How do we do that?" asked Carter.

Andrew laughed and pointed at Ana. "We don't," he said. "That's her job."

* * * * *

When everyone was back above ground, Chuck rubbed his hands and looked at Ana.

"What do you think about putting up a metal fence around the orchard? That way Ricky would have plenty of room to forage around..."

"And keep out of trouble," added Andrew as he untied the rope from the tree. "The fence would need to be at least ten feet high with a gate and a lock." Ana watched as he bundled up the rope. "That would make it more difficult for someone to get down there," he gestured with his head and then grinned at Ana. "And we could still bring Ricky the old flowers from the mausoleum, so he won't miss out on his— what did you call them—his tasty treat?" Ana gazed around at the orchard.

"That's not a bad idea," she said. "But I want the fence to be a really nice one—not some ugly chain link thing. And it needs to match the mansion."

"We'll make sure you are completely satisfied," noted Chuck.

Ana motioned back down at the dark opening in the ground.

"I want Ricky to be able to get in and out whenever he wants to." She glanced over at

Andrew. "And I want him to be safe, too." She paused and closed her eyes, "And, if it's at all possible, I want to keep…"

"Everything a secret," whispered Carter. Ana turned and smiled at him.

"Exactly."

Chapter Eighteen

As the Mercedes pulled into the driveway, Ana saw her mother coming toward them and rolled down the window.

"You two run in the house, quickly, get cleaned up and change your clothes!" Nancy waved.

"Is something wrong?" Ana opened her door and got out.

"Oh, no. Nothing's wrong," her mother explained. "We've got to go shopping! You need a new bathrobe and some other things for your slumber party."

"So, who's going to watch Connor?" asked Andrew. He turned off the motor and got out. Ana was already at the front steps but halted to hear her mother's reply.

"Oh, I shipped him off to Johnny Ralston's for the afternoon. He'll be fine."

"So, where are we going shopping?" called Ana.

"Where else?" Nancy motioned with her hand for them to hurry. "To the mall!"

Walking toward her mother, Ana asked, "Can't we wait and go tomorrow afternoon?"

Her mother shook her head. "Tomorrow we meet with Chuck. Friday you get the flowers for the Griffins' graves, and that night's your party."

"You're right," said Ana. "Well, then!" She made a goofy face, threw her hands up in the air, spun around, and shouted. "Let's go to the mall!"

Her mother followed her as she made her way upstairs to change. "It's a good thing I didn't get my hair all goofed up for Wild Hair Day, huh?" she said.

"No kidding!" replied Nancy.

* * * * *

As they made the turn to get on the bypass, Nancy placed her hand on Ana's shoulder. "Oh, I can't believe I almost forgot. Remember Mrs. Williams?"

"You mean the amazing cook you hired while you were busy cleaning up the mansion? The one who made those delicious cookies and cakes?" crooned Andrew before Ana could answer.

"Yes, Mom," she rolled her eyes at Andrew. "I remember Mrs. Williams." Ana pulled down her sun visor, so she could watch her mother's reflection in the mirror as she talked.

"Well, she's agreed to prepare all the food for your party. You and I are meeting with her and another lady, a Mrs. Fendley, tomorrow at the mansion. We can talk through the menu, the schedule, and stuff like that."

"What will Mrs. Fendley be doing?" asked Ana.

"Mainly housekeeping," responded her mother. "You know, making up beds, stocking the bathrooms, getting everything ready, helping us clean up on Saturday, and also assisting Mrs. Williams with the meals."

"Wow. You've been busy."

* * * * *

As they made the turn into the huge parking lot of the Grove Park Mall, Ana's mother received a text on her cell phone.

"Oh. This is from Diane Davis," she announced. Ana watched as her mother read the long text. "Oh, wow!" she exclaimed. "The oil paintings from the mansion have been cleaned. They want to deliver and rehang them tomorrow afternoon."

"I had forgotten all about them," said Ana. "I can't wait to see how they look now. Would it be possible for them to bring them before we meet with Mrs. Williams and Mrs. Fendley?"

"Good idea. I'll ask her."

Ana watched as her mother tapped in the request. After a minute, she smiled. "They can meet us there at 3:30 pm. Diane said it shouldn't take more than an hour and a half. I'll text Mrs. Williams and see if she can meet us at 5:00." Andrew guided the Mercedes into a free parking space.

He turned off the car and quivered all over. "Ooh! Oh, boy!" he wrinkled his nose.

"What's up with you?" asked Ana.

"I'm just so excited! I get to spend the whole afternoon, watching you shop in the mall."

* * * * *

Two and a half hours later, Ana and her mother finally headed toward the main exit. Behind them, Andrew struggled along, lugging several large shopping bags full of things that all girls' mothers think they need.

"You're only spending one night," he grumbled, "not a whole month!"

Just outside the exit door, Ana halted, dropped her bags she was carrying onto the ground, and frantically patted her pockets.

"Where's my phone?" Her facial expressions morphed from disbelief to desperation, just like everyone who has lost something valuable. For several seconds, she stood there like in a trance, desperately trying to retrace her last steps. Finally, Ana thrust both hands into the air. "I remember putting it on the shelf in the dressing room in Wilsons so I wouldn't sit on it when I tried on that cute jumper. I know right where it is. I'll run go get it." She was gone before Andrew, or her mother had a chance to respond. As she weaved her way through the crowded mall, Ana prayed without closing her eyes.

Dear Lord, please let it still be there.

* * * * *

It took Ana only a few minutes to reach the two-story department store. Nimbly weaving her way through the maze of shelves, she arrived at the section with girls' clothing. The same elderly lady in charge of the dressing rooms had just finished with a customer and smiled at Ana as she walked up.

"I think I left my cell phone in one of the dressing rooms!"

"I have it right here." The attendant opened a wide drawer. "You were in number eleven." Ana let out the breath she had been holding. The lady removed a yellow sticky note with #11 written on it and handed it to Ana.

Thank you, Lord!

"I always check the rooms after a customer is finished. You would not believe how many people forget their cell phones, coats, pocketbooks, purses, keys, or something. Why, the other day a lady left her little boy in #6."

"Did you put a sticky note on his head?"

"Ha!" laughed the lady, "I'll have to remember that one."

"Well, I appreciate you taking care of my forgetfulness," said Ana. "Thank you so much."

"Oh, don't mention it. Thank you for shopping at *Wilsons* and please come again."

"Oh, I will!"

On her way back through the store, Ana noticed the sign pointing toward the public restrooms. Immediately, she realized that she would not be able to wait until they got home.

It'll only take a minute.

Chapter Nineteen

Like in most large department stores, the public restrooms in Wilsons were clearly marked. On this floor, however, they were almost hidden from view behind some racks offering men's suits on sale. Other than a mother and her young son, who had stopped to get a drink at the water fountain near the entrance, there was no one else in the long, unremarkable hallway.

Upon finishing, Ana made her way back down the empty hall. There was no one at the water fountain.

Oh, good.

Carefully pressing the long 'PUSH' bar on the front of the fountain, she leaned over to get a drink. She recalled waiting in line at the water fountain at church. Suddenly, Ana sensed that someone had walked up behind her.

"Where did you find it?" The man's deep, sharp voice startled her. Spinning around, Ana wiped her mouth, and gasped. Lawrence Hill glared down at her from about three feet away. Recoiling in horror, Ana's back hit the PUSH bar of the fountain again, causing another stream to arc through the air.

"Find what?" she stammered, shaking her head.

"The will, of course!" he demanded and took a step toward her. "Don't play dumb with me, little girl!" Frantically glancing from side to side, Ana knew that she was trapped.

If I try to get past him, he'll grab me for sure!

"Just tell me where it was!"

Sliding to the left away from the water fountain, Ana inched backwards down the empty hall. The smartly dressed attorney held up his hands and followed her.

"Hey! Hey!" His voice was now controlled but still demanding. "I'm not going to hurt you, but I've got to know. It's driving me crazy!" Ana prayed but didn't close her eyes.

Dear Lord Jesus! Please help me! Help me!

Suddenly, an incredible feeling of peace, calm and strength hit her like a strong breeze. Ana stopped backing away, stood her ground, and began stabbing the air at him with her twelve-year old finger.

"Why should I tell you?" She leaned toward him. "You didn't care about the Griffins. You just wanted his money. That's why you had him write the will the way he did."

"How do you know about that?"

"I know everything. I know exactly what you did." Ana shook her head at him. "After he died, you spent years tearing up their home."

Lawrence Hill bit his bottom lip and glared at her. Ana changed her tone of voice to match her indignation. "But the worst of all was what you did in Lewis' bedroom! The flag that was on his casket! You just threw it on the floor like it was a piece of garbage!"

"I don't know what you're talking about!" he exclaimed holding out his hands. "Yes. I helped him write his will, but that was the only time I was ever in there!" Ana read the fake shocked expression on his lying face.

"Oh really?" she snapped. "I saw you in the mansion. Twice!" Ana held up her right hand and spread her fingers. "And I've got your fingerprints!"

"Is that a fact?" The visibly enraged lawyer started toward her, "You little, smart aleck, I'll..." He never finished. From behind, Ana saw two monstrous arms wrap around him and pin his arms to his sides. "Ahh!" Lawrence Hill yelled as his feet left the ground.

"That's it, pal!" bellowed Andrew, lifting him off the floor. "You are out of here!" He turned and carried off the horrified lawyer like he was moving a dressed-up store mannequin. Ana couldn't believe her eyes.

"Oh, Andrew! It's you!" she shouted. "You found me! Oh, praise God! Praise God!" she repeated, waving her hands in the air.

He wheeled around, slinging Hill in the process, and checked Ana from head to toe. "Are you okay? He didn't hurt you, did he?"

"No." She wanted to cry but fought back the tears. "He just scared me half to death!"

"I demand that you put me down!" Andrew's captive protested. "Do you have any idea who I am?"

"Sure. I know who you are." Ana's huge bodyguard jostled him in his arms to get a better grip as they exited the men's department and out into one of the main aisles. "You're that famous lawyer who just got himself in a whole heap of trouble."

Hill struggled for a moment like a giant stork caught in a snare, but then went limp again. "Where are you taking me?"

"Well, for starters, to the mall security office, where we will press charges against you for attempted assault on Miss Stilwell."

"That's preposterous!" Hill screamed. Andrew halted, stared at him, and then back at Ana.

"Wow! He even sounds like a lawyer, huh?" he winked at her and kept walking.

As they left Wilsons department store, Andrew didn't slow down as they turned into the flow of oncoming and very surprised shoppers. Everyone quickly got out of the way. Ana instantly remembered the famous scene from *The Ten Commandments* with Charlton Heston.

It's like God parting the Red Sea for Moses and the children of Israel!

"This is ridiculous!" Hill twisted around and glared at her. "Can't you talk to him? Tell him that I was not going to hurt you."

Ana shook her head, tossing her long blonde hair. "It sure didn't look that way to me," she called above the noise of the busy mall.

* * * * *

At the security office, Ana texted her mother to let her know where they were. Three minutes later, Nancy arrived. Huffing, she plopped down the mountain of shopping bags in a deserted corner. Turning around, she glared at Lawrence Hill and walked over to embrace her daughter.

"I'm all right," Ana assured her. "Andrew got to me in time." She pulled out her cell phone to call her father and then Chuck. After waiting over an hour, they all stood up when they entered through the glass doors.

"I am so sorry that this took so long," Chuck apologized. "Are you okay?"

"I'm fine now," Ana raced to her father and buried her face into his hug.

Ana's lawyer walked over to a plain, wooden table in the corner, opened his briefcase, and took out some papers. He directed his attention at Ana and Andrew. "Would both of you please come here and read these written depositions? I had them prepared after you called. You'll need to make certain that they describe exactly what happened and then date and sign them."

The two of them did as he instructed. Chuck inspected the papers and their signatures. "Since Ana is a minor, Ronnie, would you place your signature below hers and print 'father' to the right of it?" Ana watched as her father also signed the document. She glanced over at Lawrence Hill. His whole head was trembling like a volcano ready to erupt.

"This is an outrage!" he exploded. "I've done nothing wrong! I am completely innocent!"

Chuck glanced over to him. "Miss Stilwell and her personal bodyguard, former police detective Andrew Collins, have just signed testimonial statements to the contrary." He turned around, winked at Ana, and looked back at Hill.

"So, here's the deal, Lawrence," Chuck produced another page from his briefcase and held it up in front of the seasoned attorney. "If you sign this document, promising to stay away from Miss Stilwell and her family for a distance of at least one hundred feet," he paused for effect, "then we can settle this."

"I'll see you all in court!" Hill slammed his fist down upon the metal desk to his right.

Blang!

"You hit my desk like that again," stated the female mall security officer, sitting behind it, "and I'll make sure that you also never step foot in this mall again."

Chuck placed the paper on the desk and gestured toward Andrew. "Mr. Collins, here, says he clearly heard you threaten Miss Stilwell and saw you make a menacing move toward her." He pointed at Ana. "And from what Miss Stilwell says she told you in the hallway, you must agree that you definitely had a motive to harm her." Lawrence Hill gritted his teeth. Chuck extended both hands with palms up. "But we want this to be over. So. I'm going to offer you one last chance to come to your senses and sign this agreement."

"That would be the same as admitting I did what they are accusing me of! I'll die before I agree to that!" he bellowed.

Chuck bent over and stared him in the face. "Well, then it's your own funeral." He stood back up and waved his hands. "But look on the bright side, Lawrence. You won't have to worry about paying for it."

"What do you mean?" Hill stammered.

Chuck motioned toward Ana. "She has more than enough money to bury you!"

Andrew spoke up. "And I'm sure the security camera in the hall recorded the whole thing, too." Lawrence Hill took a deep breath, shook his head, and slowly let it out.

"Okay," he glared at Ana. "Just tell me where you found the will, and I'll sign anything you want."

Stepping forward, she glared back at him. "I'll give you one guess, so you better make it a good one."

Hill's mouth curled up with the most wicked grin Ana had ever seen.

"Talk around town is you allowed Diane Davis' bunch to clean everywhere but the cellar and his study. It was in the study, right?"

Ana wanted to scream but didn't. She gritted her teeth and faked a grin.

This is horrible! Now everyone knows!

Even though she felt like she had been kicked in the stomach, Ana was determined not to show it. She motioned to Chuck. He leaned down closer, so she could whisper in his ear.

"How silly of me! What am I going to do now?"

She held her head so that Chuck could whisper in her ear.

"Just tell him, he's right. You're still the only person alive, who knows exactly where it was."

Ana sighed and stared back at Hill. "Okay," she nodded. "I found it in the study."

"I knew it! I knew it!" he cried, looking around the room at the others. Hill started to jump to his feet but was forced back down into his chair by the security guard standing behind him. Directing his attention back at Ana, he demanded, "Where in the study was it?"

Tilting her head at him, Ana grinned. "It was right under your nose the whole time, but you were too blind to see it."

"Miss Stilwell found the will in the study," said Chuck as he removed a ballpoint pen from his pocket. He clicked it and placed it on the desk next to the agreement. "I suggest you keep your part of the bargain. This is your last chance, Lawrence. We mean it."

The defeated lawyer dropped his head and stared at the floor. After a full minute, he looked up at Ana.

"Okay," he nodded. "I'll sign it. I'll stay away from you and your family."

"At least one hundred feet away," growled Andrew.

Ana studied the lawyer's face. Suddenly, she remembered his BMW. "Which includes the estate," she paused for effect, "and the street in front of our house." Hill's head shot up again. He glared at her and then smirked.

"Yeah, sure. Whatever."

* * * * *

On the way home, no one said a word for several miles. Her father was in the front seat. Ana and her mother rode on the back seat.

"Thank you, Andrew, for protecting Ana from that horrible man."

"I can't believe I hesitated, going after her."

Ana cleared her throat. "No. It was all my fault. I never should have run off like that. I wasn't thinking." She paused. "It's just that…"

"It's just that sometimes you'd like to be like everyone else," said her father. She almost nodded but then didn't. "Is that what you want, Ana? For everything to be like it used to be?" Her Mercedes turned onto Griffin Avenue. Out the window was her stone wall. Soon, her majestic entrance gates came into view. Ana pressed her forehead against the window.

Of course not.

"Ana? Is that what you want?" he asked again.

She shook her head and sighed, "No, sir."

Chapter Twenty

While shopping in the mall, her mother had reminded Ana about Pajamas Day. Now, as she walked down the hall the next day, she was so glad they had settled on the red and black buffalo print onesie. A lot of the kids were dressed up like animals with hoods covering the top half of their faces: dogs, cats, rabbits. A teddy-bear. A pig. Others were wearing their super-hero pajamas. Connor had insisted on wearing his Spiderman pajamas, even though they were too small for him. Without warning, Skylar Perkins rounded the corner wearing a red and black, buffalo print onesie.

"Are you kidding me?" shouted Ana.

Skylar struck a pose. "I got these yesterday at the mall."

"Me, too!" howled Ana.

"Everyone will think we did it on purpose as some weird way to show that the war between us is finally over."

"I hope so." Ana put her hands on her hips. "My mother insisted I needed new pjs for the slumber party."

Skylar laughed. "Mine, too!" She pointed at Andrew who was a few feet away. "What's up with him? He's not wearing pajamas."

Ana spun around, winked at her stern-faced bodyguard, and then looked back at Skylar. "I don't think they make a onesie in his size."

* * * * *

In the car on their way to the mansion later that afternoon, Ana's mother spoke up from the back seat.

"I've got a surprise for you." Before Ana could respond, her mom motioned with her hand. "Andrew, would you please pull in at the main entrance?"

"Yes, ma'am," he responded. Ana could tell he was also as curious as she was. Seconds later, they slowed down and turned in.

Nancy Stilwell leaned forward and handed a small remote control to Ana. "Point it at the gates and see if it works."

Ana held it up and pressed the button.

"Oh, wow!" she smiled as the gates parted in front of them. Andrew guided the Mercedes slowly through the opening. When they were on the other side, Ana pressed the button again. Automatically, the gates closed behind them. Ana twisted around with an inquisitive look on her face.

"How did you...?"

"Diane Davis brought it by this morning. She wanted to make sure we were still on for this afternoon."

"This is so cool," she said shaking her head. "Won't it be fun for everyone to come in this way on Friday night?" Ana glanced over at Andrew. He was smiling from ear to ear as they made their way down the impressive, oak-lined driveway for the very first time. Ana leaned forward as far as her seatbelt would allow and gazed out the window. Soon her mansion came into view.

"Oh, look!" admired Andrew. "What a picture."

Ana nodded. "This is what the Griffins saw every time they came home."

Thank you, Lord. I'm so glad that all of this doesn't belong to Lawrence Hill.

As they reached the parking area, the car came to a stop, but Andrew didn't turn off the motor. "Why don't I go ahead and open the service entrance for Mrs. Davis and the delivery trucks?"

"We should have just left the main gates open for them," said Ana. Andrew shook his head.

"No ma'am. All deliveries must come through the service entrance. Only family and invited guests are allowed in through the main gate."

151

"Well, look who's being a snob, now!"

"I'm not being a snob," he countered. "It's a matter of security."

Ana glanced at her mother and made her wide-mouthed *I-should-not-have-said-that* frog face. She reached over and patted Andrew on the arm. "Please forgive me. After saving me from Lawrence Hill, I'm all for you taking care of my security."

Andrew grinned, "The pleasure is all mine, Miss Stilwell."

* * * * *

"Here they come, now." Ana turned to see where her mother was pointing. Three, large, plain, unmarked delivery trucks and a black SUV with a *Lewistowne Lifestyles* logo crept along the service road. "Diane said they always deliver extremely valuable pieces of art in trucks that won't draw attention," explained her mother in a hushed tone, as if she was afraid someone might be listening. Ana sighed and shook her head.

I'm twelve years old and I own three truckloads of extremely valuable pieces of art.

* * * * *

"Miss Stilwell, may I introduce Signor Antonio D'Amico!" Diane Davis was more than gushing, as she introduced the sixty-something year old

Italian-looking man who had just exited one of the trucks.

That has got to be the wildest mustache I have ever seen.

"A Miss-a Stilwell-a," he bowed. "It is-a great-a honor to finally-a meet-a you-a in-a person."

Not knowing how to respond to such a greeting, Ana thought she might ought to curtsy, but then remembered that she didn't know how. And she didn't dare look at Andrew, either. If she did, they both would lose it and die laughing.

"Uh. I am so glad to meet you, uh, Signor, uh, D'Amico," she stuttered and returned his bow.

"Oh-a, please-a! Call-a me, Antonio!"

Ana gestured with her hand. "This is my mother, Nancy Stilwell." Mr. D'Amico shook her mother's hand but didn't bow. He stared back at Ana. "And this," she turned to her right, "this is my personal assistant, Andrew Collins." Ana rolled her eyes at her bodyguard and flashed a toothy smile. Andrew stepped forward and stuck out his hand. This gave Ana a chance to signal to Mrs. Davis that she wanted her to take over the conversation. Fortunately, Diane got the hint.

"Signor D'Amico..." Diane began.

"Oh, a please-a, call-a me Antonio."

Diane smiled. "Antonio is considered to be one of the top restorers and experts of fine art in the world. He was in Italy when I contacted him about your collection." She nodded in his direction. "He was very gracious to drop everything and come at once."

"A-Please-a," the expert begged holding his two hands together like he was praying. "It is-a honor to be allowed-a to even-a touch-a such masterpieces!" He waved toward the open rear doors of the truck. The whirring of the truck's power lift transporting three of his team upward toward the treasure trove forced him to raise his voice. "This-a has been-a one of the greatest-a highlights-a of my-a career-a!"

"We are so thankful that you could come!" shouted Ana's mother over the noise. "Thank you so much!"

"Why don't we go inside," gestured Diane. Everyone, except the Italian art expert and his team, followed her suggestion.

* * * * *

"Why are they all wearing rubber gloves?" asked Andrew.

"Most people don't realize," explained Diane, holding up her hand, "that our skin has a natural oil on it. If I touch a painting without first washing my hands with soap and water, I'll leave a tiny smudge on it. Over time that oil collects dust and dirt." Ana rubbed her middle finger against her thumb.

Well, at least Lawrence Hill's nasty old fingerprints aren't all over them anymore.

She remembered how he had pushed the larger paintings to the side in his desperate search for Mr. Griffin's lost will. The smaller ones, he had taken down and leaned against the wall—without caring to rehang them. Now, Ana watched in amazement as Signor D'Amico's team went about their separate tasks with precise coordination.

Wow! These guys are pros!

As each painting, now stunningly restored to its original brilliance, was unwrapped and put back in place, it was welcomed with an appropriate chorus of *oohs* and *aahs*. Signor D'Amico explained, with a great deal of fanfare, which master painted it, and when, and why it was so important.

Ana leaned over to her mother while his back was turned away from them and smiled. "Why aren't we filming this?"

* * * * *

After an hour and a half, all the paintings were finally back where they belonged. Ana and her mother escorted Signor D'Amico, his team, and Diane to their vehicles, thanking them for the excellent job.

Standing in front of the mansion, Ana offered her hand to the Italian art aficionado, expecting him to shake it. Instead, he bowed, gracefully took her tiny hand in his, and lightly kissed it. "Please-a Miss Stilwell," he gushed. "Do not hesitate to-a call-a me if I-a can-a be-a of any further-a service to you-a."

"Oh," stammered Ana. "Of course. Thank you. Thank you so much." She shot Andrew a glance and mouthed: "Do something."

Stepping forward, he said, "Signor D'Amico, would you and your team please follow me? I'll open the gate for you." He moved toward the Mercedes.

"Uh, Andrew," called Nancy. He stopped and spun around. "Would you please wait and let Mrs. Williams in? She and Mrs. Fendley should be arriving any minute."

"Yes, ma'am." Ana and her mother waved goodbye as the column of trucks and the black SUV drove away. For a moment, the two of them stood quietly.

"At least now you know everything about the paintings." Nancy grinned. "If any of the girls or Mrs. Thompson has a question about one, you'll be able to… "

"Oh, good night!" exclaimed Ana. "There's no way I can remember all of that. Do you think Mrs. Davis has a list of who painted what, and when, and why?"

"Probably." She put her arm around Ana and gave her a little squeeze. "But if not, I'm sure

Antonio would be more than willing to come back and do it all over again."

Ana used her fingers to curl a wild, make-believe mustache. "And he-a would-a be the highlight-a of my-a whole-a party!"

Chapter Twenty-One

"I am so excited I can hardly stand it!" Margaret Williams beamed as she got out of her car.

"And we are so glad you could come," said Nancy. When they got closer, their former cook introduced her friend, LeAnn Fendley. Ana extended her hand.

"It's so nice to meet you."

The short, stout, cheery Mrs. Fendley grabbed Ana's hand and shook it firmly. "Oh, believe me, Miss Ana," her eyes glistened, "the pleasure is all mine."

She has got the kindest, happiest face I have ever seen.

Once inside, Ana enjoyed listening to the glowing, unrestrained reactions of the two older ladies as they made their way across the entrance hall.

"Let's go upstairs to the second floor and see the rooms where the girls will be sleeping," suggested Nancy. Ana was glad that her mother was taking the lead. Mrs. Fendley pulled out a small notebook and began writing. Because no one would be sleeping on the third floor, there was no need going up there.

Back on the first floor, the group viewed the large parlor where the girls would meet and also the formal dining room where the meals would be served. As they walked past the smaller, private family dining room, Ana slowed down and looked inside. Her mother, the two ladies and Andrew kept making their way ahead of her down the hall. Standing in the doorway, she was glad that they had nixed the idea to eat in there.

I could just see Olivia Freeman finding the hidden button on the underside of the chair molding and asking: 'What's this for?'

"Now this! This is what I call a kitchen!" proclaimed Mrs. Williams. Ana rushed to rejoin the tour. Mrs. Fendley was still in the hall and turned toward Ana. Her eyes were sparkling.

"Your whole mansion is like being in a dream."

"I'm so glad you're here," Ana replied. She hoped that her eyes were sparkling, too.

Nancy stepped forward. "Would you like to prepare the food for the party in here? Everything has been cleaned and restored, so it all works perfectly."

"Are you serious?" The professional cook who just weeks before had concocted all kinds of delicacies for the Stilwell family turned and nodded at her friend. LeAnn Fendley was excitedly nodding her head up and down and grinning from ear to ear. "Oh, we would love to!" Behind her, Andrew mumbled something. Ana knew exactly what he wanted.

"Mrs. Williams?" she grinned. "Would you bake one of your delicious caramel fudge cakes for the party?"

She nodded. "I hoped you would ask."

"Uh!" Ana's bodyguard chimed in from the doorway. The sheepish look on his face was hilarious. "Since I'm not invited," he stared at Ana and then back at Mrs. Williams, "could you maybe bake two of them? Please?"

Ana shook her head at him. "You're coming to the party. You can sleep in one of the extra bedrooms on the first floor."

Mrs. Williams walked over and opened the door to the exquisite, industrial-sized oven. "I was planning on baking several cakes to make sure you have enough for all of your guests."

"That's what I'm talking about!" hooted Andrew, clapping his hands. The rest of the arrangements went smoothly and before long, Ana, her mother, and Andrew were headed home.

"We can't forget to save a couple of pieces of cake for Connor," noted Ana.

"Oh, I'm *so* glad you remembered!" exclaimed her mother. "If we forgot and he found out, he would never forgive us."

* * * * *

That night, as Ana was standing in her closet, trying to decide what she could possibly wear for Throwback Thursday, she spied the boxes of Beatrice Griffin's diaries on the floor. She hadn't touched them since discovering the clue about Castle Greifenstein. In fact, that same book was still lying on top of the others just like she had left it. Ana shook her head.

Mr. Griffin didn't even know she wrote these.

Sitting cross legged on the floor, Ana opened the book, and began flipping through the pages until she found the place where Beatrice had mentioned Rudolph wanting to buy the castle.

Closing her eyes, she tried to recall her conversation with him the night before he died. She remembered praying for him and him showing her the envelope with the new will, but there was something else. Something about the diaries.

"I told him that they were like a record of their whole life together, and…" she muttered and then let out a muffled squeal. "And then he asked me if I had read all of them. Oh, my goodness!" Ana clutched the diary to her chest. "That has to be why he gave me the *See-if-you-can-SNIFF-this-out* note! Since Beatrice wrote about everything, maybe he figured that she must have mentioned something about him, Lewis, and Douglas digging another tunnel!" She glanced at the book in her hands. "If that's true, then that would mean it was dug while she was still alive!" Ana laid the diary onto the floor.

I need to put this one down and go back to where I stopped reading them in sequence.

She glanced at the box.

I've got to search all of them.

* * * * *

Leaning backwards, so she could see the clock on her nightstand, Ana could not believe that time had passed so quickly.

1:13 a.m.

"Just a little longer," she groaned, "it's got to be here somewhere." To her right was the stack of diaries she had already checked. She had decided to focus only on the words *tunnel, cave* or *digging,* but it was proving to be a challenge because Beatrice was a very interesting writer. Now and again, Ana discovered something about the family she really wanted to know and would keep reading, sometimes for several pages. And even though she was loving every minute of it, more than once she had to scold herself.

Stop it! You can always read them in detail at another time!

* * * * *

It was almost 2:30 am, when Ana paused to check the time again. With her finger inserted in the book to hold the place, she glanced at the edge to see how many pages were left. She was a little over half-way through.

Okay. I'll finish this one and then call it quits for the night, uh morning.

After a serious yawn, she stretched and casually flipped the page. The word *digging* grabbed her attention like a speck of gold in a miner's pan.

"Finally." Ana sat up straight and read quietly out loud:

> *"This morning, Rudolph stuck his head in the room to say that they are digging again. I told them to please be careful. That means he will also let the staff go. Again. It used to bother me, but now I'm accustomed to seeing people come and go. Rudolph is determined to keep everything a secret. The main thing is that he's happy. I'm glad he and Lewis enjoy spending time together."*

Her eyes begged for sleep but stopping was out of the question. Feverishly she plowed through volume after volume. Nothing. One diary was left in the box. She glanced over at the second box which she hadn't even touched yet. Ana took a deep breath.

I'll quit after this one.

163

After maybe twenty pages, she sat up, rubbed her eyes, and read out loud:

> *"Tonight, during dinner, I asked Rudolph how their new project was coming along. It has been several months now, and I have actually enjoyed cooking again. I am thankful for the day maids, but I miss having staff in the house. Rudolph said "The Lair" was almost finished. That's what they call it. He said it also gives them another way to get out...whatever that means."*

Ana quickly searched through the rest of the book. There was no more mention of digging, tunnel, or The Lair.

I wonder what a lair is.

She carefully put all the diaries back in the box. Standing up, she stretched and yawned.

Mom would really let me have it if she knew I was still up.

After closing the door to her closet, Ana went to her desk and picked up her cell phone. Finding the dictionary app, she typed in: *lair*. Along with other definitions, the words: hideaway, hiding place, hideout, cache, shelter, retreat, hidey-hole were also listed.

"Oh, my, goodness!" she squealed.

It's not just a tunnel. It's another room! A hideout. Their secret hidey-hole! And it's got another way to get out of the mansion without being seen. Which means it could be connected to Ricky's Palace.

After turning off her phone, Ana crawled into bed, and clicked off her lamp.

Ricky tapping his nose on the wall has got to be what Mr. Griffin wanted me to sniff out. The question is: Where is the entrance to The Lair?

Chapter Twenty-Two

"Wow! Look at you!" approved Ronnie Stilwell the next morning as his twelve-year old daughter entered the kitchen.

"Not bad, huh?" Ana struck a pose. She was wearing a 1970's style, black and white plaid, pleated skirt; a white, collared, button up shirt; long white, knee-length socks; and black and white saddle oxford shoes.

An hour earlier, her mother had miraculously retrieved the ancient ensemble that had belonged to her grandmother, Pam, from a trunk in the attic. Ana sashayed over to the counter, dropped two pieces of whole wheat bread into the toaster, and pressed down the lever. Leaning over the top of the toaster, Ana watched as the heating elements began to glow. She liked it only lightly toasted, so she was waiting on just the right moment.

"Ana?"

"Yes, sir?" she answered without turning around. Her father winked at Nancy, who was sitting across the table from him.

"What do you think about inviting Carter and his family over to the mansion on Saturday afternoon for a late lunch after your slumber party guests are gone?"

Ana whirled around. "Are you serious? Really?"

"Sure. Why not?" Her mother smiled.

"That would be absolutely amazing!" Their suggestion was totally unexpected, but also totally fabulous. Ana was now convinced her parents were the two coolest people on the planet.

"We figured you might like the idea, so I went ahead and called the Hudson's. They're excited and it's all set." Stunned, Ana watched as her mother poured Apple Jacks and milk into a bowl. Nancy continued, "I also asked Mrs. Williams and Mrs. Fendley if they wouldn't mind making lunch for all of us and then joining us." Ana plopped down on the chair closest to her. "After that," Nancy smiled, "we'll sit around the pool, and whoever wants to can go swimming."

"I want to go swimming!" bellowed Connor as he bounded into the room. Sliding into his chair, he began gobbling down his breakfast. "Where are we going swimming?"

Still in a daze, Ana mumbled. "The estate."

"Yippee!" he garbled past a mouthful of cereal. "I have been dying to do a cannon ball off that diving board!"

Ding!

Two pieces of very dark toast popped up out of the toaster.

* * * * *

Unlike her school in Braxton, the Lewistowne Elementary school, because it was the oldest one in town and was huge, also housed the middle school for Ana's district. In fact, the students were only separated by a set of double doors. So, even though technically Ana was already in middle school, no one seemed to make a big deal of it.

Carter Hudson, however, did make a big deal out of the fact that Ana was wearing a skirt. He had never seen her in one before, especially not one like this.

Nodding his head, he gave his approval. "Wow! You're uh, uh..." Whirling around, Ana held out her hands, palms down, so that they skimmed the surface of the soft, cotton cloth.

"Pretty?"

"Uh, yeah," he grinned. "You're pretty."

Carter blushed and Ana whirled again.

I love Throwback Thursday.

* * * * *

That afternoon, Ana watched through the glass sidelight of their front door as Chuck got out of his truck and made his way toward their front porch.

What's with him?

She opened the door and repeated her question as he got closer. "What are you smiling about?"

"Good afternoon to you, too, Miss Stilwell," he countered as he ascended the steps. Instantly, Ana felt ashamed for greeting one of her most trusted friends in such a childish and cheeky manner.

"Oh, yes. Please forgive me. Good afternoon to you. How are you doing?"

Chuck snapped to attention. The genuine expression of joy returned to her financial advisor's face.

"Ecstatic!"

"Really?" Ana extended her hand in friendship. "Have you got some good news?"

Chuck reached out and gave her much smaller hand a firm shake. "Oh, yes. Some very good news."

Later, sitting around the table in the living room with her parents, Ana watched as Chuck produced copies of the weekly financial statement of her fortune.

"You asked me to come up with some ideas about using half of your money, which amounts to approximately two hundred million dollars, to help poor people find good-paying jobs."

Ana wasn't expecting Chuck just to blurt out her plans and watched her parent's reaction. If their eyes had bugged out any further, they would have popped right out their sockets and rolled across the floor. She felt like she should say something by way of explanation and looked back and forth at her mom and dad.

"I got the idea from reading the Bible in Sunday School," she said. "That's what Zacchaeus did after he met with Jesus."

"Zacchaeus was a tax collector who had robbed the people," said her father. "He was just paying back what he stole from them."

"Dad!" Ana stretched out her hands with her elbows resting on the table. "He gave back four-times what he had stolen and then half of everything he owned to the poor." She sat back in her chair and crossed her arms. "I figured if some old tax collector that got his heart right with God could give half of what he had to help the poor, why couldn't I do the same thing with half of the money I've got?"

Ronnie glanced over at Ana's mother for help. Nancy stood to her feet and then threw up her hands.

"Oh no! This is a catastrophe!" She looked at Ana and winked. "Our rich daughter wants to spend half of her money creating good-paying jobs for the poor. How ridiculous is that? She must have lost her mind!" Nancy walked over, leaned down, and kissed the top of Ana's head. "That's what we get for giving our daughter a Bible and taking her to Sunday School"

"I'll still have about two hundred million dollars left," Ana said and glanced over at Chuck. "Right?" She noticed the odd smile had returned to his face, but now it looked even goofier than before. She rolled her eyes at him. "What is it?"

Chuck tapped on the financial report he had handed out. "Your fortune is always increasing because of dividends you receive on a regular basis from some of your stock holdings. See the line that says Dividends?" He pointed. "See the total of your dividends at the end?"

Ana looked at the bottom of the list of stock symbols and the corresponding dollar amounts. "Oh wow! It's over a million dollars!"

"Uh, huh," Chuck said. "Now look below them at the line that says Sale of Stock. See the symbol and the amount next to it?"

The three Stilwell's dropped their heads to gaze at the sheet. Nancy started cackling with laughter. Ronnie sat in stunned silence. Ana stared at the amount: $207,155,431.06

"Are you serious?" she cried.

Chuck laughed. "Yes, ma'am." He read the amount out loud, "Two hundred and seven million, one hundred and fifty-five thousand, four hundred and thirty-one dollars and six cents."

Ana looked at him and held out her hands. "What happened?"

He grinned. "One of the companies you don't control, but in which you are heavily invested, meaning you own a lot of stock—I mean a lot of stock. Well, another company just bought it out." He pointed at the figure. "And that is what they paid you for your shares."

"Did I have to sell my stock?"

"In this case, yes."

"Why?"

He smiled. "Because they made the company an offer they couldn't refuse." Instantly, Ana remembered wanting to buy the two houses and property belonging to their neighbors.

"So, was it a good deal?"

"Oh yes!" Chuck laughed, held up the paper and shook it. "It was a very good deal!"

Ronnie Stilwell rubbed his face with his hands. "This is unreal!" he muttered. "No matter how much money Ana gives away, the Lord just keeps sending her more!" He glanced around at the others. "Can we pray? I want to ask God to forgive me for acting… silly."

After her father's prayer, Chuck laid out a proposal on the table with the title *Ana*

Stilwell's Jobs Initiative. It was basically a list with stuff like researching the most feasible and best possible types of good-paying jobs, the education and training which would be required, locating and determining which people would be recruited to fill the positions, what kind of facilities or workspace would be needed, support for families with children, working out all the permits and governmental regulations and requirements, and many other items. Ana sat quietly for several minutes studying the proposal.

This is unreal. This is going to be much harder than I realized. What am I going to do?

No one said a word. Finally, Ana spoke up. "I want to help poor people, but this…" she held up the piece of paper, "this is going to be a ton of work. Do you really think we ought to do it?"

Chuck took a deep breath, let it out, and grinned. "Sure. Why not?"

"Do you think two hundred million dollars will be enough?"

"Well, it will certainly be a start." He laughed and leaned toward her. "When other people, people who have much, much more money than you do, young lady, when they hear about what you're trying to do, well, don't be surprised if they want to be a part of it, too."

Without warning, Andrew stuck his head through the living room door.

"Are you guys going to take a break soon?"

Ana could tell that he was getting tired of dealing with her little brother. Her mother jumped to her feet.

"Yes! Let's take a break!" she exclaimed. "I baked a deep-dish apple pie and bought a half gallon of vanilla ice cream to go with it."

"Hallelujah!" cried Andrew.

Chapter Twenty-Three

The hot topic of discussion on the last day of school, at least among the girls, was the slumber party that evening at Ana's mansion. Skylar made it clear to everyone that it was an exclusive occasion. Ana overheard her telling one group of girls, "Only members of our Sunday School class are coming."

Some of the girls stated they were going to start attending the class the following Sunday and asked what time it began. "At 9:00 a.m. sharp, and you'll need to be on time!" Skylar barked. "And be sure to bring a Bible with you. But please don't come if you are not serious about learning God's Word!"

Ana shook her head. *Pastor Barnes would love this. He's always encouraging us to be bold witnesses for Jesus.* She looked at the faces of the girls. *But Skylar takes bold to a whole, new level!*

* * * * *

That afternoon, after placing the fresh, new flower arrangements on the Griffins' graves, Ana and Andrew took the old ones to the orchard and dropped them on the ground near the trap door.

"If Ricky gets used to eating these here, maybe he won't get confused when we put up the fence," she said.

"It was wild the way he crawled straight to that spot in the wall down there and started tapping his nose against it," recalled Andrew.

"Oh, I forgot to tell you," said Ana. "There is definitely another room with a tunnel that might lead to Ricky's Palace."

"Are you serious?"

Ana nodded. "Uh, huh. Beatrice mentioned it in one of her diaries. She wrote that Mr. Griffin told her they were digging it to have another way out."

"So, the entrance has got to be somewhere inside the mansion," he exclaimed.

Ana nodded. "That's what I figured."

Rubbing his chin, Andrew asked, "Where do you think it is?"

Ana shook her head. "I don't have a clue."

*****

That evening, Andrew insisted on receiving Ana's guests at the main entrance.

"Please be nice," Ana pleaded.

"I'm going to say, 'Welcome to the Griffin Estate and Mansion.' Then I'll check their identity against the list of your classmates' names and give them some simple instructions."

"Just don't scare them to death. I know that on the inside you are a great, big, lovable teddy bear, but on the outside, you can be pretty intimidating."

Shaking his head, Andrew puffed out his chest and then burst out laughing. "Please don't ever call me that again."

"What?"

"A great, big, lovable teddy bear."

"Well, that's what you are."

* * * * *

Each of the girls and Mrs. Thompson arrived on time. As their parents helped them out of their vehicles with her backpacks, Ana smiled and asked that each girl remain on the front steps. "Mom wants to take a photo."

The plan was for the parents to just drop the girls off without going inside.

"They'll want to take a tour of the mansion and won't want to leave," Ana's father had joked. He had been in the mansion several times while it was being restored.

Nancy had also suggested that the group should enter the mansion together, so that each girl could have the same experience of seeing it for the first time. It was a good idea.

Ana had so much fun watching the different reactions as they walked through the beautiful front doors. Shouts of amazement, eyes wide open, hands over mouths, pointing, laughing, and staring in every direction. Courtney Thompson was the last to enter.

"Oh, my word!" she exclaimed. "This is unbelievable!"

Ana walked to the center of room and held out her hands. "Welcome. I am so glad you all could come." The excited group of girls broke into spontaneous applause. Ana smiled and gestured with her hand toward the magnificent grand staircase. "Please get your things and begin making your way up to the second floor and I'll show you to your rooms." Letting the girls and her teacher go ahead of her, Ana listened to their loud and lively chatter as they ascended the staircase. Skylar Perkins walked over and stood beside Ana.

"So, who's the poor soul that's going to be stuck in a room with me?" Ana turned, stared at her, and broke into the widest grin.

"Me."

"You? Really? Are you serious?" Ana enjoyed the expression on Skylar's face as she stepped backwards and dropped her backpack on the floor. "What are you doing? Keeping your friends close and your enemy closer?"

Ana walked over, picked up Skylar's backpack, and put her arm around her shocked classmate. "How did you guess?"

Skylar howled with laughter. "I am so glad you let me come. This is going to be a lot of fun!" As the two of them climbed the stairs, Ana voiced a silent prayer.

Yes, dear Lord. Please let it be fun.

* * * * *

"There are nine, almost identical bedroom suites on this floor," Ana explained as her Sunday School class paid close attention. "Tonight, we will be using six of them. Two girls to a suite. Your names are on the doors." Excitedly, the girls began checking for their names and jabbering at the top of their lungs.

'Can you believe this?' 'Oh, wow!' 'You've got to be kidding me!' and other similar expressions of joyous surprise echoed repeatedly throughout the cavernous hall.

Courtney Thompson had not moved from the top of the stairs and was enjoying watching the girls. Ana walked over and touched her on the arm. Pointing to the door directly behind them, she smiled. "Your suite is the middle one. It's a little larger than the others, and it's all yours."

As she opened the door, Ana's teacher shook her head. "Oh, my goodness! This is gorgeous!" She turned and gave Ana a quick hug. "Thank you so much for inviting me. I have been so looking forward to it."

"It wouldn't be right for our class to be together without you."

"You are kind to say that." Mrs. Thompson placed her overnight bag on the floor. "Where will you be sleeping tonight? Upstairs?"

"Uh, no." Ana hesitated. "I'll be on this floor with everyone else."

I need to change the subject fast.

Ana backed out the doorway and onto the balcony. She motioned with her head over her left shoulder. "I'll be sharing a room with Skylar. I'll, uh, I'll see you downstairs after you get unpacked. Don't forget to wear your pajamas." Ana managed a weak grin. "This a slumber party, remember?"

Courtney Thompson laughed. "I'm all prepared." Ana gave her a thumbs up and headed toward her room.

I sure hope she's not going to be wearing a red and black, buffalo-print onesie that she got at Wilsons.

She wasn't, but Skylar was. "Hurry up and get changed into your pj's!" cried Ana's roommate as she entered their room. The lively talk from the other girls walking around in their pajamas was increasing in intensity. Skylar looked at Ana. "Is it okay if I don't wait for you?"

"Oh, sure. You go ahead and have a good time getting to know the other girls."

While she was changing, Ana wondered how long it had been since the Griffin mansion had been this alive.

Chapter Twenty-Four

A delicious dinner was enjoyed in the main dining hall. The magnificently arranged table had lighted candles, the finest, white China, and gleaming sterling silver place settings. Above the girls' heads glistened four exquisite Italian crystal chandeliers. When they were finished, ten stuffed, happy girls and their Sunday School teacher made their way to the parlor that had been set up for their meeting.

"Who would like to open our meeting with a prayer?" asked Mrs. Thompson. Ana looked around the room and was about to raise her hand, when…

"I will!" Maggie Benson, who was sitting on the other side of Skylar spoke up. All the girls bowed their heads. Half-way through her prayers, Ana peeked at her.

Huh?

Maggie was holding on to Skylar's hand. Ana closed her eyes and listened as she prayed.

"And Lord, thank you that we can always trust You, no matter what. In your name we pray…"

"Amen!" All the girls ended the prayer together.

Ana saw Maggie glance around the room. She sensed that something was up because Maggie was still holding Skylar's hand.

"Our newest class member has an important announcement." Maggie turned and winked at Skylar. Ana's former enemy stood to her feet. Her hands were trembling.

"I got saved!" she blurted out and then burst into tears. Maggie stood up and put her arm around her. After a moment, Skylar quit shaking and continued, "I asked Jesus to save me, and He did!" She glanced over at Ana. "And believe me, I really needed it!"

Leaping to her feet, Ana thrust her arms around Skylar. Both girls began crying. Everyone stood up and surrounded them, crying, and hugging, and jumping, and just enjoying the moment.

After congratulating Skylar and offering a prayer of thanksgiving, Ana's teacher explained, as simply as she could what "being saved" and "being a Christian" meant. Every girl had either a serious question or a personal comment. Mrs. Thompson always referred to Bible passages for the answer. Ana could tell that each of the girls was desperate to know "the truth." Two hours passed unnoticed. Finally, Nancy stuck her head in the door.

"Ready to head back to the dining room for dessert?"

"If you mean some of that cake we've been smelling?" Olivia Freeman gazed around the room. Every head, including Mrs. Thompson's was nodding. "Yes, ma'am! We are ready!"

* * * * *

Ana had just put the last bite of cake in her mouth when, Caroline Jensen, one of her more daring and inquisitive classmates got up and walked toward her.

I wonder what she wants.

Out of the corner of her eye, Ana noticed that all the girls were watching Caroline.

"My mom wanted to know if you were going to give us a tour of your mansion."

Ana swallowed the bite, emptied her glass of the last mouthful of milk, smiled at Caroline, and stood up. She didn't have to get everyone's attention because she already had it.

"After everyone is finished, uh, if you want, I'll show you around."

"Move it!" yelled Olivia. It was like she fired a starting pistol. She and the other girls, including Ana's teacher, began cramming in the last morsels of the insanely delicious cake into their mouths and guzzled down the last drops of whatever they were drinking. Someone should have timed them because without a doubt, they set a new world record in speed eating. After cleaning up and wiping their mouths, all the girls gathered quickly at the door to the dining room.

"Follow me," gestured Ana. Behind her, excited talk commenced. It didn't stop until she did in the middle of the main entrance hall.

"This," she began, pointing with her hands in every direction as she talked. "This was the home of Rudolph Mason Griffin, his wife, Beatrice, and their son, Lewis." Ana stopped and shook her head.

Well, what do you know about that?

The sound of the words coming out of her mouth, talking about the Griffins, felt so natural, so right. She stared at the wide-eyed faces studying her every move, hanging on to her every word. Chuck was right. She didn't need to be afraid of anything. Ana grinned.

This is going to be fun!

Amazingly enough, she was now actually looking forward to giving her Sunday School class a tour.

As Ana began telling the story of the Griffins and the history of Lewistowne, everything fell into place. Interesting facts she had discovered in the old newspapers were woven together with personal tidbits she had gleaned while reading the diaries. You would have thought she had written the words down and had rehearsed them for weeks. But she didn't have to. Ana knew it all by heart.

All of the rooms that opened onto the main entrance hall were explored with the exception of the study. Ana had remembered to lock the door when she got to the mansion before her guests arrived. She had immediately put the key onto the ring with the skeleton key and the key to the door that gave access to the cellar. Now, as she continued the tour, Ana felt the ring with the keys in the right pocket of her pajamas. She usually hid the others in her underwear drawer at home when she wasn't in the mansion.

Where can I hide these? I don't need to keep them with me tonight!

"Oh, Ana!" exclaimed Mrs. Thompson as they exited the music room. "This is so amazing. I never knew that Lewistowne used to be named Pineville. You must know more about our town and the Griffins than anyone!"

Ana smiled. "Oh, I don't know about that. Before, in school, I never really liked to study history, but I do now." Saying the word "study" made her think about Mr. Griffin's study. She jammed her hand in her pocket to hold the keys to keep them from jingling as she walked.

While making their way down the carpeted hall past the four rooms where Mrs. Williams, Mrs. Fendley, her mother, and Andrew were staying, Ana directed the group's attention to the windows on the left that allowed them to see the indoor garden. It had been cleaned up and replanted with all sorts of ornamental shrubs, trees, and flowers. Turning to the left, they proceeded down the rear service corridor.

"This first room on the right was the break room for the staff." Ana opened the door and turned on the light. She stepped into the room and waved her hand around, while the girls and Mrs. Thompson watched from the doorway.

"Look at that old TV!" Olivia shouted.

"It is over forty years old," noted Ana. She showed them the cabinets on the right side of the room. When she turned back around, her gaze fell on fifteen to twenty keys hanging on a long rack just to the left of the door. Most of them appeared to be typical house keys, but a couple were old type skeleton keys. Ana grinned.

Where is the best place to hide keys that you don't want anyone to find? With other keys."

Everyone was obviously done with the boring break room and were milling around in the hall.

"The rest of the rooms on the right are just storage," she explained. "Please keep going until you get to the huge grandfather clock." As the group moved off, she quickly pulled the keys out of her pocket, hung them on the rack, clicked off the light, and closed the door.

Ana watched as the group passed the place in the wall where the secret passageway lay hidden behind the paneling. She had decided to not show them any of the "more interesting" aspects of the mansion.

187

Interestingly enough, none of the girls asked her to reveal how she got into the mansion in the first place. After seeing the small private dining room, they stuck their heads into the fabulous kitchen where Mrs. Williams and Mrs. Fendley were still cleaning up. They stopped to show the girls and Mrs. Thompson the amazing pantries. After thanking them, the group returned to the main hall.

* * * * *

On the second floor, where they were spending the night, Ana told them about the lavish parties and the famous guests that the Griffins had hosted.

Bethany Green, who had beautiful long blonde hair like Ana, piped up, "You mean they slept in the same rooms where we're sleeping tonight?"

"That's correct."

"Do you know who slept where?" asked Olivia. "In which bed?"

"No," Ana said. "They didn't write that down. Or if they did, I haven't found it, yet."

"Well, keep looking!" hooted Olivia as she looked around at the other girls. "I would love to know if I'm sleeping in the same bed where Judy Garland slept! You know, Dorothy in the Wizard of Oz!"

Now, everyone began jabbering excitedly, wondering who of the other famous people Ana had mentioned had slept in their beds.

Ana waited patiently for the chatter to die down without saying a word. One by one the girls stopped talking and turned to look at her.

Ana narrowed her eyes at them and lowered her voice. "Now, we go this way."

She led them to the bottom of the staircase. Placing her hand on the wooden banister, she paused and looked at them one by one.

"Only a very few people have ever seen what I am now going to show you. Be careful and stay together. And please, please do not touch anything."

Ana slowly climbed the stairs.

"What's up there?" Olivia asked.

Ana turned and stared at her. "The Griffins' private bedrooms."

Chapter Twenty-Five

The steps creaked and groaned as they slowly climbed the stairs. At the top, Ana waited until everyone had made it.

"On these walls," she motioned to the right and then to the left, "are personal family photos. They were taken on special occasions and on many of their private trips and vacations."

After giving the group enough time to look at the pictures and make comments, Ana continued to the only door on the right side of the long wall.

"This was the bedroom of Rudolph Griffin. You are free to look around the room, but please do not touch anything." Ana opened the door and stood quietly as the group filed past her into the room.

"Good night!" roared Skylar, flinging out her arms in front of her. "Now this is what I call a bedroom!"

"You can say that again," remarked Olivia.

"Look at that bed!" exclaimed her teacher. "It's like something out of a movie."

"Ana? Have you ever spent the night in here?" Amy Edwards wanted to know.

"No," Ana shook her head. "Not in here or anywhere else. Tonight, is my first time to actually sleep in the mansion, too."

"She's sharing the room with me," announced Skylar proudly.

As her guests made their way around the enormous room, Ana slowly walked over to the gigantic window on the opposite side. After several minutes, she invited everyone to join her. "If you will all come over here, I want to show you something."

Gazing downward, Ana directed their attention to the imposing structure in the middle of the lawn. "That is the Griffin family mausoleum." Even though the sun was almost gone, there was still enough glow to light up the brilliant copper door. "It's made of Carrera marble Mr. Griffin had imported from Italy. He built it for his beautiful and beloved wife when they found out she had cancer." Ana turned and motioned to the opposite wall. "Photos of her are over there." Turning back around, she continued with her story. "Beatrice Griffin died many years before he did, as did their only son, Lewis. Now, they're all buried inside. Notice that the mausoleum is the focal point of the landscaping."

"My mother said that Rachel Bennett told her that you pick up six hundred dollars' worth of roses every other week," declared Charlotte Howard. "She told my mom you put them on their graves. Is that true?"

Everyone stared at Ana. "Yes. Mr. Griffin made sure there were always fresh roses on their tombs." Ana tilted her head and placed her hand lovingly on the window. "I figured it was the least I could do as a way to remember and honor them." After a moment, everyone quietly went back to examining the room.

"Wow! Look at the painting of this castle!" called Bethany Green excitedly. Ana turned and walked toward her. All the girls and Mrs. Thompson joined them. "Is this a real place?"

"Oh, yes" pointed Ana. "If you'll look closely, you can tell that it is actually a photo that was made to look like a painting."

"Do you know where it is?" asked Mrs. Thompson.

"Yes, ma'am," said Ana. "It's in a small village just west of Vienna in Austria." She almost touched the painting with her finger. "That's the Danube River."

"Wow," all the girls cooed in unison.

Back out on the third-floor balcony, Ana walked over to the rail. "If you are not afraid, come see what it looks like from up here." She smiled and pointed downwards. Most of the girls joined her, gazed down, and voiced their amazement. Amy, Bethany, and Charlotte, however, held hands and slowly inched their way toward the others. About two feet from the rail, they stopped.

"This is close enough," Amy announced with Bethany and Charlotte nodding their heads in agreement.

After viewing the family entertainment room on the left side of the wrap-around balcony, Ana led the group to Lewis's bedroom, opened the door, and held up her hand.

"Please just look into his room from the doorway. It's been completely restored to the way it was when Lewis was alive. The only difference is the flag in the frame on the wall directly above his bed. That's the flag that was draped over his coffin."

Ana's teacher was the last to gaze into the room. "He is the one meant by the word "Hero" in the name of your newspaper. And that's why his photo is on the front page of every issue, isn't it?"

"Yes, ma'am," she nodded. "He was a real hero. I'm going to do whatever I can to make sure he is never forgotten."

"Amen." Courtney Thompson reached over and placed her hand lightly on her shoulder. Ana looked up at her.

"If Lewis had not sacrificed his life in Vietnam to save others," she swallowed, "then this mansion and everything else would have belonged to him."

"Well, I think they all would be proud of you."

"I sure hope so."

Turning around, Ana noticed that all the girls had returned to the center of the balcony. Suddenly, she remembered what was next on the tour and stared up at her teacher.

"I need to tell you something in private before we go any further," she whispered. Ana softly explained in her teacher's ear the truth about Beatrice Griffin's bedroom. When she got to the disturbing part, Courtney Thompson pulled away. Her pretty face had contorted into a mixture of astonishment and dread.

"You have got to be kidding me!" she mouthed.

"I wish I was," winced Ana, motioning with her eyes over her shoulder at her classmates. "What do you think I should tell them?"

"Well, what you just told me is going to make me lock my door tonight and read my Bible until I fall asleep," sniffed her teacher. "Why don't you just show us the rooms but don't tell *everything* you know about them."

"Now, why didn't I think of that before?" muttered Ana.

"I wish you had!" snorted her teacher. "Oh, how I wish you had!"

Leading the girls to the right side of the huge hall, Ana explained, "These last two rooms belonged to Beatrice Griffin. The first one is her private parlor and office, and the second one is her bedroom suite."

The girls oohed and aahed at the amazingly gorgeous rooms, and almost freaked out at the fabulous walk-in closet. Ana's teacher didn't utter a peep but kept staring at the bed. On the way back down the stairs to the bottom floor, she waited behind the others so that she could talk to Ana.

"And when you entered her bedroom for the first time, how long had it been locked up?"

"Between forty and fifty years. I don't know exactly. It was pitch dark in there until Mom and I opened the drapes and the shutters to let the light in. I'll never forget seeing it for the first time all covered in dust and cobwebs." Ana considered telling her teacher about the diaries, but then didn't.

"And you say Mr. Griffin never when back in there after she...died?"

"Yes, ma'am." Ana stopped on the stairs and stared at her. "There were medicine bottles and a spoon still on the nightstand. You could see the stains on her pillow and even the impression where her head had been."

"Stop! That's enough!" Courtney Thompson threw up her hands. "I'll have to call my husband to come sleep with me tonight if you say another word." After a few more steps, she shook her head. "I am SO GLAD that you did not tell the girls. They would never make it through the night! We would have to call their parents to come and get them!"

"Tonight was only the third time that I've been in there myself." Ana shuddered all over and then laughed. "I plan on reading Psalm 23 over and over tonight until I drop."

"Amen to that," mumbled her teacher.

Chapter Twenty-Six

For the next hour, the girls told stories and played games in the parlor.

"Can we play hide and seek?" asked Olivia. All the girls were for it.

"Sure," said Ana. "But only on the first floor. Just be careful and remember not to touch anything, especially the paintings. And don't run around because you might knock something over." All the girls stared at her. "Good grief," groaned Ana. "I sound like my mother." Everyone laughed and promised to be careful. After several turns of being "it", they all returned and plopped down on the floor of the parlor.

Katie Strong, the tallest girl in their class, asked if she might try out the grand piano in the music room.

"Oh, that's a great idea," approved Ana.

"Only if she knows how to play," joked Mackenna Myers as she and all the girls made their way into the adjoining room. Katie took her place at the piano and quickly proved that she did, in fact, know how to play. Beautiful classical music echoed through the mansion. After several selections, Caroline Jensen spoke up. "Can you play something fun?"

Katie grinned. "You mean like this?"

As soon as she began, everyone howled, "The Chicken Song!" They sprang to their feet and started wiggling.

"I remember this one," said Mrs. Thompson. She joined them but soon gave up. "I'm just not as coordinated as I used to be." The girls enjoyed singing, wiggling, and laughing. When the large grandfather clock in the library let them know that it was midnight, however, one by one they began to run down.

"I'm going to bed," announced Olivia Freeman.

Katie, her roommate, stood up from the piano. "Me, too."

"Why don't we straighten up down here and meet at the bottom of the staircase for prayer?" suggested their teacher.

Minutes later, everyone, including Ana's mother, Mrs. Williams, and Mrs. Fendley, stood silently in the grand hall as Ana prayed out loud. After saying good night, they all headed toward their respective rooms.

"I'll make my rounds and stay up for a while until everyone is asleep," announced Andrew. Courtney Thompson walked over and thanked him personally for being there and watching out for them. "Oh, it's my pleasure. Sweet dreams." Ana heard her teacher mutter something under her breath but couldn't understand what it was.

* * * * *

"So, what were you and Mrs. Thompson whispering about up on the third floor and on your way back down the stairs?" garbled Skylar. She was standing in the doorway to the bathroom with her toothbrush stuck in her mouth.

"If I tell you, you'll have nightmares and won't sleep a wink," said Ana. Skylar disappeared back into the bathroom. Seconds later, she reappeared, turned off the bathroom light, and climbed into her bed.

"Try me," she grinned. "I'm a big girl. I can handle it. Anyway, now that I'm saved, I'm not afraid of going to hell anymore. Praise God! I am going to sleep tonight, safe in the arms of Jesus."

Ana smiled. "I am so glad you told us. I know I won't ever forget it."

"How old were you when you got saved?" asked Skylar.

"Ten and a half. I was at a church camp back in Braxton where we used to live."

"What happened?"

"We had Bible studies every morning and worship every evening, so I had time to think about it a lot and ask questions." Ana sat up on the edge of her bed. "One of our counselors told me that I was making everything too difficult. And I was." She looked over at Skylar. "So, I prayed to Jesus and thanked Him for dying for me. I accepted His salvation and He saved me."

"That's almost exactly what Maggie told me after church. I prayed to Jesus and gave Him my whole, rotten life. My sins. My mouth. My being so jealous of you." She stared at Ana. Skylar shook her head. "If you hadn't gotten my dad that job at your newspaper, then we would never have started going to your church." She leaned up on her elbow. "Why don't people go to church? It's wonderful."

"Beats me," said Ana.

"Probably because they don't know Jesus like we do, huh?"

"I guess." Ana realized that she needed to start inviting people to worship. For several minutes the two girls lay quietly listening to each other breathe.

"So, are you going to tell me what you and Mrs. Thompson were talking about?"

"Nope."

"Why not?" prodded Skylar.

"Because now, believe it or not, I kinda' like you. And I don't want to give you nightmares." Ana laughed. "If you were still a mean, horrible jerk, then I would tell you. But now you're my...my sister in the Lord, and I want you to be happy and have a good night's sleep."

"You're serious, aren't you?"

"You better believe it! Good night sister Skylar!" sang Ana.

"Talk about being sneaky."

* * * * *

Shortly after 7:30 the next morning, the sound of doors opening and shutting mixed with the wound-up, happy conversations of twelve-year old girls echoed through the mansion. Ana shook her head.

Well, so much for the notion that all "almost teenagers" like to sleep late on Saturdays!

Lying flat on her back, Ana put her pillow over her face.

"Are you awake, yet?" whispered her roommate.

"Are you kidding?" Ana pointed at the door without removing the pillow. "How could anyone sleep through that?"

"Oh, come on!" laughed Skylar, who was now standing next to Ana's bed. "Who wants to sleep? This place is insane!" Ana stared up at her. Skylar's eyes were as wide open as saucers. "Everyone, and I mean, everyone in Lewistowne would just die to be in here!"

Ana threw back her covers and jumped out of bed. "Well, then, come on! Let's go join them."

* * * * *

After a delicious breakfast and a very lively Bible study, everyone got dressed. Ana led the group on a stroll around the grounds of the estate. Andrew went with them. At the edge of the overgrown orchard, she introduced them to Ricky who was busy munching on some flowering vines. Andrew snapped a group photo of the girls and Mrs. Thompson with the ancient pet.

After a swim in her pool to cool off, everyone got dressed again, packed up, and assembled once in the main entrance hall to wait on their parents to pick them up.

"I'm so glad you could come." Ana and her mother waved from the front steps to the departing families and Ana's teacher.

"Is there any of that cake left?" Andrew begged from behind them.

"I think so," Nancy winked at Ana. "You'll have to check in the kitchen." He took off jogging in that direction.

"I thought you were going to help us clean and straighten up everything before Carter's family gets here!" called Ana.

"I will! I will!" he waved without looking back. "I promise!"

* * * * *

Later that afternoon, with the mansion all cleaned up and after a delightful lunch, Ana's parents, the Hudson's, Mrs. Williams, and Mrs. Fendley sat around the sparkling pool. Everyone seemed to be having a great time. Well, almost everyone.

"Why can't I get in?" pleaded Connor. He was already standing on the diving board. Ana could hear him from inside the pool house where she was changing into the brand-new swimsuit they had purchased in the mall.

"Because you can wait on your sister and her guest," explained her mother. Ana shook her head. She knew he wouldn't give up that easily.

"But why? It's only Carter."

"You can wait until your sister says that it's okay to get in." Ana recognized her father's voice, growing in intensity with each word. "You got me, pal?"

"Yes, sir." Seconds later, Carter, and Andrew emerged from the door on the left side and Ana walked out of the one on right side.

"Okay," Ana smiled and waved at her younger brother. "Show us what you've got!"

"Yippee!" Connor took off running, bounced into the air, and screamed, "Cannonball!" The resulting splash did not make it out of the pool.

Ana was next. She performed a simple dive, head-first into the water, and swam to the side of the pool to wait for Carter.

"Show 'em how it's done!" called Carter's father. He grinned at the others. "Watch this!"

"Don't embarrass him, dear," cautioned Carter's mother.

Carter grinned, held up his hand and put it back down. Carefully, he made a steady, well-trained approach. Ana saw the end of the board bend downwards under his weight and then launch him high into the air. Her mouth fell wide open, as he perfectly executed one and a half somersaults with a half-twist. As his body knifed into the water everyone clapped and cheered.

"That was amazing!" Ana cried as his head broke the surface of the water. He joined her at the ladder. "Where did you learn to dive like that?" Carter grinned and motioned for her to go ahead of him.

"We've got a pool behind our house," he laughed. "It's nothing like this one, but it does have a diving board."

Andrew was next.

"Do a cannonball!" Connor yelled.

"Coming right up!" responded Ana's very large bodyguard.

"We all might need to move back," Ana's mother suggested. Everyone gasped as Andrew got airborne.

"Geronimo!" he hollered. As he hit the water, everyone was thankful they had heeded Nancy's warning.

After about a half-an-hour, Ana grabbed a towel, wrapped it around her, strolled over, and stood in front of her mother. "Do you mind if I show Carter the inside of the mansion? He hasn't seen it since it's been cleaned." Nancy glanced over at Ronnie and Carter's parents. They all smiled and nodded.

"Sure," Nancy approved. "Have fun." She glanced at the pool where Connor was begging Ana's bodyguard to toss him up into the air again. "We'll let Andrew know where you are."

"Thank you," Ana said as she reached down and hugged her mother.

Still drying his head with his towel, Carter walked up next to her. "What's up?"

"Would you like to get changed and go see the inside of the mansion?" Ana grinned, put her finger across her lips, and motioned at the pool.

Carter laughed. "You better believe it. I can go swimming any old time."

Chapter Twenty-Seven

Ana opened the front door to the mansion and let Carter enter ahead of her.

"Oh, wow! Wow! Wow!" he exclaimed as he strolled into the center of the main entrance hall. "This place is fabulous!" He grinned at her and bowed deeply. "My lady."

"Give it a break," she muttered. "Come on. Let me show you around."

As they passed the door to Mr. Griffin's study, Carter stopped and tried the latch. "Why is this one locked? What's in here?"

"Are you kidding me?" Ana laughed out loud.

"What?"

"I'll explain it to you later."

She turned and took off in the direction of the rear service corridor. Carter was close behind her.

"Where are we going?"

"To get the key!" she called over her shoulder. At the huge ornamental vase, where she had hidden and got her first glimpse of Lawrence Hill, Ana paused. "Mr. Hudson, you are fixing to get the grand tour. Deluxe!"

* * * * *

After retrieving the keys from the staff's break room key rack, the two of them hurried back to the door of the study. Inserting the key, Ana unlocked it and pushed it open. The last time she had been in there was with Chuck and Andrew. Nothing had changed.

"Oh, my word!" remarked Carter. "This room is a dusty wreck."

"The whole place used to look like this before it got cleaned." She closed the door behind them.

"Why didn't you have them clean in here?"

She moved to the center of the room, turned around, and held out her arms for effect. "Because this is where I found Mr. Griffin's will."

"Oh, wow!" Carter swallowed hard.

Going to the other side of the dark mahogany desk, Ana sat in the executive leather chair. The notepad with *Hill, Rayburn, and Johnson* embossed across the top, the one she had used to figure out the combination to the safe was still lying where she had left it. Looking down at her feet, Ana recalled cowering beneath the desk and praying that Lawrence Hill wouldn't catch her.

I don't have to worry about him anymore.

She glanced up at Carter, who was obviously still processing the treasured secret that she had just revealed to him. Puffing up his mouth and lips like he was blowing out a candle, he slowly let out the breath he had been holding.

What's he thinking? Does he want me to show him where the will was? Do I dare?

Over his shoulder, Ana glimpsed the huge family portrait on the wall. She got up and walked over to the painting, the only one in the whole mansion that had not been restored. Carter quietly followed her every move.

For a minute, she stood motionless studying it. A smile slowly spread across her face.

Yep. Mr. Griffin is still staring down to the right at Ricky's head poking out of the bushes.

This had been the crucial clue. It had led her to concentrate to the right at the window on the opposite side of the room. A small, thin lever concealed in the intricate frame opened a hidden door beneath the window. Behind the door was the safe containing the lost will.

Ana sighed and began examining the exquisite, gold gilded frame of the huge family portrait.

"Oh, my goodness!" she shouted.

"What?" cried Carter. "You scared me half to death!"

"Sorry." Reaching out, Ana rubbed the left side of the frame up and down with her hand. "I can't believe I never noticed this before!"

"What?"

"It's not hanging on the wall." She turned, stared at him, and pointed. "See? It's built into the wall!" Stepping back, she examined it from the front. "He couldn't take this one down or push it to the side to check behind it. I'll bet that drove him absolutely nuts!"

"Who are you talking about?" asked Carter.

"Lawrence Hill."

"The lawyer?"

"Uh, huh," she nodded and moved closer to the painting. "He helped Mr. Griffin write his will." Bending over, she studied the bottom of the frame in detail. "Then after Mr. Griffin…" she glanced up at Carter and rolled her eyes, "died, Hill broke into the mansion and then spent years searching for it."

"How do you know that?" he asked.

"I saw him."

"You saw him?"

"Uh huh." Ana's nose was almost touching the frame. "Twice."

"Are you serious?"

"Yep. I had to know who else was in here, messing up the place. The second time, he almost caught me hiding underneath Mr. Griffin's desk over there."

"Oh, my goodness," exclaimed Carter. "Weren't you scared?"

"Petrified," she chuckled. Ana stood back up, wiped her hands, and looked at Carter. "But Lawrence Hill was not supposed to find the will. I was. I am convinced that God wanted me to find it."

"What do you mean?" he asked.

"Think about it." Ana stepped back to get a better look at the whole frame. "God let us move here and buy the house where we live. He used me being such a loner that I spent most of my time playing in the creek." She held up her fingers and counted off the steps. "He used me being such a snoop that I spent hours going through the town's old newspapers, researching the Griffins. He let me find the tunnel. And the way into the mansion. He helped me not to chicken out, even though I told myself a thousand times I was crazy."

Carter laughed. "Okay, okay. I believe you. God did it."

Ana went back to examining the frame.

"He also used my keen ability in knowing how to keep a secret," she mumbled without looking over her shoulder. Carter cleared his throat but didn't respond. Ana kept rubbing the frame with her hands, searching to determine if a hidden lever was embedded in the ornate molding. After a couple of minutes, she groaned, stepped back, and stood next to Carter.

"This doesn't make any sense."

"Maybe there's nothing to find," said Carter.

Ana shook her head. "No. It's here somewhere. It's got to be."

"How can you be so sure?"

"Because God helped me understand how Rudolph Griffin's brain worked. How he liked to hide things." Suddenly, it came to her.

It can't hurt to try.

Walking over to the right side of the painting, Ana leaned her head against the wall, just like she had done so many times before.

"What are you doing now?"

"I'm being Ana Stilwell," she grinned. The right side of the frame was now less than a foot away from her face. Painstakingly slow, she inched her gaze up and down.

All I have to do is see it. Something odd, out of place. A tiny lever. A button. The clue you want me to find. Where is it?

211

"See if you can SNIFF this out," she muttered softly.

"The message on the card," said Carter.

Ana moved her head out, away from the wall, to reposition herself. The light pouring in through the large window on the opposite side of the room reflected off the front of the painting. Instinctively, her eyes quickly scanned across the lighted surface.

Huh?

A single, small, round smudge caught her attention. Ana thought about what Diane Davis had told her.

Someone must have touched it with their finger.

Keeping her focus on the position of the smudge, Ana slowly moved to the left until she could tell where it was on the painting.

"Good night!" she screamed. "Look! It's on Ricky's nose! Ha! Let's see what this does." Carefully but firmly, she pressed on the spot with her thumb. A low whirring, mechanical sound came from behind the painting.

Ker-clunk!

The massive frame popped slightly away from the wall on the right side to reveal a large, dark, empty space behind it.

"What on earth?" cried Carter.

"This is so Rudolph Griffin! It was right here all the time!" she clapped. "Thank you, God!" She eased the frame farther open to the left and stuck her head into the opening.

"Oh, wow! There's a narrow passageway that leads off to the right. It runs behind this wall with the bookcases." Ana stepped behind the painting, turned to the right, and disappeared into the darkness. Carter was right behind her.

"Hey! You're blocking the light." she fussed. "I can't see!"

"Sorry!" He stepped back out into the room. "How's that?"

"Much better! Thank you."

After a moment, he called. "How far does it go? Can you see anything?"

"Hold on!" Seconds later, she poked her head back out through the opening. "It looks like there's a spiral staircase at the end of the passageway."

"Oh, wow!" he exclaimed. "Which way does it go? Up or down?

Ana smiled and motioned with her finger. "Down."

"Yes!" Carter clapped as she stepped back out into the study. "Do you think it leads to Ricky's Palace?"

"There's only one way to find out." Placing her hands against the frame, Ana carefully pushed it back into place. Again, the faint whirring sound ended with...*Ker-clunk.*

"There's got to be a heat sensor that triggers the locking mechanism," he proposed.

Ana didn't respond. She just stood there, staring at the painting... at Ricky's nose.

Well, Mr. Rudolph Griffin, I sniffed it out.

"So, what do we do now?" asked Carter.

"What do you think?" She bugged her eyes at him and grinned. "We go get my flashlight."

Coming Soon...

Book #5 in the Ana Stilwell Series.

ANA STILWELL

The Lair of the Treasure Hunters

Gift Offer

Thank you for choosing J. W. Jenkins' latest Ana Stilwell book. We hope you enjoyed it. We'd like to express our appreciation by offering two free books.

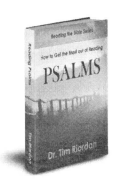

Dr. Tim Riordan has written a book to help you learn how to read and study the book of Psalms. You will find it to be a useful companion to his other book on Psalms: *Songs from the Heart: Meeting with God in the Psalms*. To receive your pdf copy, please visit

Greentreepublishers.com/free-gift---psalms.html.

Judah Knight a novella as a companion to his *Davenport Series*. The series is written for adults, but it's safe for the whole family. This novella takes the reader back to the teen years of the two main characters. Request a free copy of his novella entitled *A Girl Can Always Hope* by visiting judahknight.com/free-gift.

More Books from GreenTree Publishers

Wisdom Speaks: Life Lessons from Proverbs
By Tim Riordan

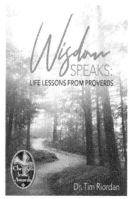

Have you ever wished for a "How To" book on life? God has given us one in the book of Proverbs. Join pastor and Bible teacher Dr. Tim Riordan on a journey through this book of wisdom where you study one of the most read books of the Bible. Through Proverbs, wisdom speaks. Are you listening? Chosen for the Christian Indie Award in 2019.

Following Jesus: A 21-Day Journey
By Tim Riordan

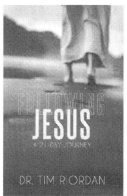

Following Jesus: A 21-Day Journey is a guide to help you experience Jesus and grow in your faith. Some say it takes twenty-one days to make a habit. This book will help you develop the habit of a daily quiet time and deepen your prayer life.

Not only will you experience twenty-one days of Bible study on various topics leading to spiritual growth, but you'll also enjoy an allegory that introduces each section. This story will lead you to think of important principles for your own spiritual journey.

A Walk in the Woods
By Kurt Bigbee and Nori Kimura

Zeke and Riley began a quiet hike, but the peace and silence of the woods was interrupted by a loud motor and crashing noises. At first, it looked like the beautiful forest was being cut down and destroyed. Mommy explains it's possible to harvest a forest without killing it. They see that some harvested areas are growing seedlings and showing signs of new life. They also learn loggers leave trees in some areas to protect streams. A walk in the woods is a fun adventure story that teaches the concept of stewardship, that people can utilize resources and take care of the land at the same time. Interactive activities await little learners at the end of the story to help reinforce these concepts.

> To purchase any of our books or to get more information, go online to greentreepublishers.com.

Made in the USA
Columbia, SC
11 December 2021